⬦ W9-BWG-610

Dear Reader;

The story you are about to read is perhaps the most intense and graphic portrayal of God's love that I have ever written. But I think that's a good thing. The darkness that the light of Christ came to defeat wasn't a small thing, yet the power of his glory was superior by far. So it is in this story of God's overwhelming love.

In so many ways the work of World Vision mirrors the incarnation of God's love into a world of suffering. Every child held in darkness is precious, as you will see, and in so many ways, their hope rests in those willing to bring them home.

I urge you to take this journey with Marci as she discovers the intoxicating power of Christ's love in a world where the least among us become the greatest and where the disadvantaged and suffering rule with Christ. Do so, and I promise you'll never look at this world the same again.

Thank you

# THE MARTYR'S SONG
## 30 HOUR FAMINE EDITION
### A GREAT COMPLIMENT TO YOUR WEEKEND!

Hard Cover Edition Shown

A Great Read...

Short and Motivating...

Discussion Questions Included...

FREE! Download of 'Martyr's Song' by Todd Agnew
(use download code 2006MSsong)

**WORLD VISION SPECIAL EDITION ONLY $2**

| PRODUCT DESCRIPTION | PRODUCT CODE | PRICE |
|---|---|---|
| **THE MARTYR'S SONG** Special Edition/No CD | 1-5955-4162-4 | **$2.00** |
| **VALUE PACK** 15 Copies of the Special Edition | Special Unit Pricing for Multiples of 15 Only | **$1.25** |
| **THE MARTYR'S SONG** Hard Cover PLUS CD Single | 0-8499-4499-6 | **$16.99** |

## LIMITED TIME OFFER WHILE SUPPLIES LAST...ORDER TODAY!
**Phone and Web Orders Only using MasterCard or Visa. No Mail Orders.**
Orders Ship Within 2-3 Days for Estimated Delivery in 1-3 Weeks.
For International, Puerto Rico, and Canada Orders, Please Call 615-899-9000

## Online at www.teddekker.com/MSorders
### or Call Toll Free 800-933-9673

# PRAISE FOR TED DEKKER'S NOVELS

"What an emotional and thrilling story within a story! Ted's approach allows you to see faith in a whole new light."

—MAC POWELL, Third Day

"Ted Dekker paints a picture that will create a longing in each of us to be with our heavenly father."

—DEBBIE DIEDERICH, National Director, 30 Hour Famine, World Vision

"*The Martyr's Song* drives home the realities of standing for your faith in a world where it isn't always the easy decision. It is a unique story that will keep you reading from start to finish."

—MIKE YODER, Director of Church Programs, World Vision

"[In *Obsessed*] an inventive plot and fast-paced action put Dekker at the top of his game."

—*Library Journal*

"[In Obsessed] author Ted Dekker brilliantly weaves two years—1944 and 1973—and two locations—the United States and Germany—into an exhilarating thriller of passion and hope."

—*Christian Retailing*

"With the release of *White,* and the culmination of the Circle Trilogy, Dekker has placed himself at the fore of Christian fiction. His tale is absolutely riveting, and the redemptive value at the heart of the series only makes it all the more remarkable."

—MICHAEL JANKE, *CM Central*

"One of the highlights of the year in religious fiction has been Ted Dekker's striking color-coded spiritual trilogy. Exciting, well written, and resonant with meaning, *Black, Red,* and now *White* have won over both critics and genre readers . . . An epic journey completed with grace."

—Editors, Barnes and Noble

"Dekker is a master of suspense and even makes room for romance."

—*Library Journal*

"Full of heroic action, deep meaning, and suspense so palpable your fingers will dig grooves into the book's outer cover, *Red* magnifies the story of *Black* times ten, raising the stakes to epic proportions. But Ted Dekker's biggest ace in the hole is that he understands what so many others never realize: substance and meaning *can* go hand-in-hand with exciting, cinematic storytelling. *Red* is a thrilling, daring work of fiction that not only entertains—it inspires. Why aren't there more stories like this?"

—ROBIN PARRISH, editor,
*Fuse Magazine, www.FuseMagazine.net*

"*Black* has to be the read of the year! A powerful, thought-provoking, edge-of-your-seat thriller of epic proportions that offers great depth and insight into the forces around us."

—JOE GOODMAN, film producer, Namesake Entertainment

"Ted Dekker's novels deliver big with mind-blowing, plot-twisting page turners. Fair warning—this trilogy will draw you in at a breakneck pace and never let up. Cancel all plans before you start because you won't be able to stop once you enter *Black*."

—RALPH WINTER,
Producer—*X-Men, X2: X-Men United, Planet of the Apes,*
Executive Producer—*StarTrek V: Final Frontier*

"Put simply: it's a brilliant, dangerous idea. And we need more dangerous ideas . . . Dekker's trilogy is a mythical epic, with a vast, predetermined plot and a scope of staggering proportions . . . *Black* is one of those books that will make you thankful that you know how to read. If you love a good story, and don't mind suspending a little healthy disbelief, *Black* will keep you utterly enthralled from beginning to . . . well, cliffhanger. *Red* can't get here fast enough."

—*FuseMagazine.net*

"Just when I think I have Ted Dekker figured out, he hits me with the unexpected. With teasing wit, ever-lurking surprises, and adventurous new concepts, this guy could become a real vanguard in fiction."

—FRANK PERETTI

"[With THR3E] Dekker delivers another page-turner . . . masterfully takes readers on a ride full of plot twists and turns . . . a compelling tale of cat and mouse . . . an almost perfect blend of suspense, mystery, and horror."

—*Publishers Weekly*

"Ted Dekker is clearly one of the most gripping storytellers alive today. He creates plots that keep your heart pounding and palms sweating even after you've finished his books."

—JEREMY REYNALDS, Syndicated Columnist

# THE MARTYR'S SONG

## OTHER BOOKS BY TED DEKKER

Obsessed
Black
Red
White
Three
Blink
Thunder of Heaven
Heaven's Wager
When Heaven Weeps

*with Bill Bright:*
Blessed Child
A Man Called Blessed

*Nonfiction:*
The Slumber of Christianity

# THE
# MARTYR'S
# SONG

## TED DEKKER

WESTBOW
PRESS

A Division of Thomas Nelson Publishers
*Since 1798*

visit us at www.westbowpress.com

Copyright © 2005 Ted Dekker

All rights reserved. No portion of this book may be reproduced, stored in a retrieval system, or transmitted in any form or by any means—electronic, mechanical, photocopy, recording, scanning, or other—except for brief quotations in critical reviews or articles, without the prior written permission of the publisher.

Published in Nashville, Tennessee, by WestBow Press, a division of Thomas Nelson, Inc.

WestBow Press books may be purchased in bulk for educational, business, fund-raising, or sales promotional use. For information, please e-mail SpecialMarkets@ThomasNelson.com.

Publisher's Note: This novel is a work of fiction. Names, characters, places, and incidents are either products of the author's imagination or used fictitiously. All characters are fictional, and any similarity to people living or dead is purely coincidental.

### Library of Congress Cataloging-in-Publication Data

Dekker, Ted, 1962–
  The martyr's song / Ted Dekker.
    p. cm.
  ISBN 1-5955-4162-4 (Special Edition)
  ISBN 0-8499-4499-6 (hard cover)
  I. Title.
PS3554.E43M37 2005
813'.6—dc22                                    2005001470

*Printed in the United States of America*
05 06 07 08 09 — 6 5 4 3 2 1

Dear Reader,

The novel you're about to read is an adaptation and expansion of the story Ted first touched upon in the initial pages of the novel *When Heaven Weeps*. If you've read *When Heaven Weeps*, you'll discover a familiar yet brand new story within these pages. You'll hear for the first time the actual Martyr's Song—a new song recorded by Todd Agnew just for this novel. I suspect you'll be overwhelmed at the power of that song and the far reaching impact this song of heaven has in Marci's life.

There is no order to the Martyr's Song novels—you may read the four novels (*Heaven's Wager, When Heaven Weeps, Thunder of Heaven,* and *The Martyr's Song*) in any sequence. Each story stands alone and in no way depends on your knowledge of the others.

Nevertheless, if there is one book to start with, it is *The Martyr's Song* . . . the story that came out last but that started it all.

Publisher
Westbow Press

# CHAPTER ONE

ATLANTA, GEORGIA, 1964

EVE ANGLED the old VW toward the curb alongside the high-school yard and slipped the shift stick into park. She stared directly ahead, lost in another world, nearly oblivious to the hundred or so students on the lawn to her right.

She recited the words so firmly etched in her mind as if she had written them herself.

"The soldiers stood unmoving on the hill's crest, leaning on battered rifles, five dark silhouettes against a white Bosnian sky, like a row of trees razed by the war. They stared down at the small village, oblivious to the sweat caked beneath their tattered army fatigues, unaware of the dirt streaking down their faces like long black claws."

Eve stopped. To think that it had all started so innocently. Just five tired soldiers staring at a peaceful village . . .

Someone yelled, and she turned her head to look at the students through the passenger window.

*Wake up, old woman. You're here now, not there.*

She was here to deliver a dozen of her rarest roses—crossbred Russian reds—but she couldn't focus on the task. Her mind was lost in this other world, where things like roses and cars and students meant something very different than they did here.

She was once as young as these students, fifty or sixty years ago. She'd fumbled through adolescence and come out reasonably sane, though that was before she learned the true meaning of life in that surreal moment when her world stopped for an hour or so. She found her sanity then, all of it, in a time of horror and beauty.

"Father, forgive them, for they know not what they do."

She pushed open her door and stepped out.

"Forgive them, for they simply do not, cannot, will not know—"

Eve's vision froze.

Her left foot was planted on the street, her right on the Volkswagen's floorboard. Her heart was halfway through a beat; her lungs were half-full of air. For a long moment, they stayed that way.

A girl stood alone on the lawn, staring at the other students as if unsure what to do with herself. The school, with all of its activity, faded from Eve's view.

The girl was all she could see. A girl she knew.

But it wasn't possible! Not here!

Eve's heart crashed, and the familiar rhythm of life resumed. She was mistaken. No matter how the girl resembled . . .

The girl still stood on the grass, unmoving. The other students swarmed by, but this one lost child, an outcast, shut off from the busy world around her, was immobilized by her own insignificance.

A knot of empathy rose in Eve's throat.

She'd come to deliver flowers, but she decided then that she would deliver something more.

So very, very much more.

MARCI STOOD on numb legs, unable to move. It wasn't that she didn't have the strength to walk across the schoolyard and up those wide, sweeping steps that led into the gaping double doors. It was that she didn't want to walk past the other students.

But school was out, and she had to get to her locker, simple as that. Which meant she had to pass by *them*.

She'd long ago stopped thinking of them by name. It wasn't Kevin, the quarterback who led his fans around campus, or Cheryl, his girlfriend, who had an annoying habit of popping her gum, or Tom, who had that loud motorcycle they called an Indian. It was just *them*.

There were twenty-nine kids in the eleventh grade. Twenty-eight of *them* were going to Kevin's fall party tonight. One was not. It didn't take a rocket scientist to know which one.

The one with the long, stringy brown hair. The one who had fat fingers and stubby nails. The one who tried to cover her zits with makeup but failed miserably. The one who wore Salvation Army rejects because she couldn't afford real clothes from Rich's department stores.

Marci stood still, knowing that even now, standing alone on the front lawn, she stuck out like a wart. It was Friday. School was out. She couldn't just stand here forever.

Marci lowered her eyes to the grass and forced herself forward. Her red plaid kick-pleat skirt hung around her knees. She'd saved up for three months and bought it a week ago, but she hadn't worked up the courage to wear it until today. A stupid, stupid, stupid thing to do. What was she thinking? She hated herself for feeling like she had to wear it to fit in.

Three girls were walking by, looking at her.

"Nice skirt," one of them said.

Marci's face flushed. She should have gone home.

"Stunning," the second said.

"You wearing that dress tonight?"

Marci's vision clouded with embarrassment. All of them knew she hadn't been invited.

"Never too late to impress the boys," the third said, winking.

"Please, she isn't even going. And if she showed up in that, we'd

have to lock her in the bathroom to keep the boys from throwing up."
The girl skipped ahead. "Come on! Bobby's waiting."

Marci's world spun. Funny how it never got easier. She walked forward. The steps had emptied. She climbed them a step at a time, hating every swish of her skirt.

The building had emptied too. She turned down the long hall and walked quickly, scuffed shoes clicking on the concrete floor. She reached her locker. Pulled it open and stared in.

Her diary sat on her upper shelf. She stared at it dumbly. The words she'd written just a week ago ran through her mind. *I'm pretty sure I have enough money for at least a new skirt, the one in the window at Lerners. Maybe a new blouse too! I'm going to do it! I'm going down to pick out a skirt that all the others would wish they had bought. Then I'm going to wear it to school.*

Marci reached for the diary, pulled it out. Maybe she should take the book home and burn it.

Someone was in the hall to her left. A shadow in the corner of Marci's eye. She turned her head.

A woman with gray hair, wearing a yellow-flowered dress, stood alone in the hall twenty yards away, looking directly at her. A vase of roses sat on a cabinet next to the woman.

Normally Marci would have looked away, but for some reason she couldn't. She just looked back into the woman's long, haunting stare.

They seemed to be trapped in each other's eyes. The air suddenly felt too thick to breathe. Still the woman wouldn't break off the stare. Marci didn't know what to do.

The woman was suddenly walking down the hall. Straight for her. Eyes locked.

A small wave of dread swept through Marci's chest. The woman stopped five feet away. There was something about the woman's eyes. Pity. Maybe horror. But that wasn't it. There was more.

Something surreal. Something impossible.

"What's your name, child?"

The woman's voice was soft and low with a foreign accent.

"I'm not here to hurt you," the woman said. "You may call me Eve. What is your name?"

"Marci."

"Hello, Marci." The woman blinked. "You hate yourself because you don't think you're beautiful, is that it?"

At first the question sounded distant. How did the old woman know that? Was it so obvious? Then again, people always assumed that ugly people hated themselves. Though for Marci, it was true.

"Do you believe everything can change in the space of one breath, Marci?" the woman asked.

Marci stood frozen.

The woman slipped a card from her purse. "You think physical beauty is important? Fine. I'll work in your world, for your sake.

Come to my flower shop tomorrow, and I will make you beautiful."

Marci's thoughts collided. Now that she thought about it, the woman was saying that she really *was* ugly. Of course she was ugly; everyone knew that, but not so ugly a stranger would walk up to her and make a point of it.

The woman stepped forward and slid the card under the diary's cover with a touch as soft as her voice. "More beautiful than you can possibly imagine," she said. Eve lifted her hand, touched Marci's chin. "And I'm not speaking of inner beauty, child. I can change the way you look with a power beyond your comprehension."

Then the woman turned and walked down the hall. She stepped through the doors to the street and was gone.

Marci stood by her open locker, diary in arm, staring after the woman. The first hints of real anger prompted a faint tremor in her fingers. The anger swelled to rage. How could a total stranger dare make such a cruel insult?

How could anyone walk up to her and tell her that she really *was* ugly and needed to be changed? And how could the witch taunt her with such an absurd promise? *Let's dress you up and pretend you're beautiful and parade you around the block for all the boys to laugh at.*

The tremble ran to Marci's heels. She clenched her hand, and for the first time that day, a tear slipped from her eye.

*I hate you. I hate you, I hate you, I hate you! I will cut my wrists before I come to your pathetic little flower shop!*

# THE MARTYR'S SONG

# CHAPTER TWO

EVE STOOD in the small greenhouse attached to her home and hummed as she pruned the roses. To her left, a bed of Darwin hybrid tulips blossomed bright red and yellow along the glass shell. Behind her, against the wall, a flat of purple orchids filled the air with their sweet aroma. A dozen other species of roses grew in neat boxes.

But none was so special as this one rosebush at her fingertips. This one spoke of true beauty. Magical beauty.

This was Nadia's rose, and if the unsuspecting residents of Atlanta knew the power Nadia wielded, they would . . .

The doorbell chimed.

Eve set her scissors on a table next to the book. She paused, staring at the red cover, which depicted a man's face stretched open in a throaty laugh. *Dance of the Dead*. Bittersweet. Through the right lenses, just sweet. Magic. She reached out and touched the cover. Power. So much power.

The bell rang again.

Eve let her fingers linger one second longer, then headed toward the front. She pulled the door open.

The girl stood there—Marci—dressed in the same pleated skirt and gray blouse she wore yesterday.

"How dare you!" Marci spat. The girl glared for a full ten seconds, started to say something, then clamped her mouth shut. Evidently her planned speech wasn't rolling off her tongue as intended. She turned on her heels and headed down the driveway.

"It's your decision, Marci," Eve said. "But if you enter my house, I'm quite certain you'll leave a different woman."

That stopped the girl. She didn't turn at first, and when she did, her eyes were still angry.

"Why are you doing this to me?"

"Doing what, child?"

"Lying to me! You don't even know me!"

"Then give me a few minutes and I will know you. Is your life so full of adventure and appointments that you can't spare an hour to test me?"

Marci stared at her, caught off guard.

"You came to be made beautiful," Eve said, "and I really can make you beautiful. You think this is a fairy tale? No, I'm talking about something more real than your own pain. It's not every day I offer it to someone as unappreciative as you."

They traded stares for another five seconds. *The girl is more stubborn than I guessed. Perhaps she won't succumb to the power as easily as I imagined.* Though most did. Most certainly did.

"It's your choice, Marci. But I'm not going to stand out here forever. I have things to do."

Eve started to turn back into the house.

"How do I know you won't do something crazy?" Marci asked.

Eve faced the girl and smiled. "Depending on how you see it, everything I do is crazy."

Another five seconds.

"Inside?" Marci asked, looking past Eve.

"Yes, inside."

"Okay, five minutes."

"No, it'll take an hour."

Marci hesitated. Then she walked past Eve, into the house, and stopped in the living room.

Eve closed the door. "Do you smell that?"

Marci looked around and saw the roses on the bookcase to her left.

"Nadia's flowers," Eve said. "They smell sweet, like gardenia blossoms, but they're actually roses. Nadia is the one who taught me what I will show you. Please sit down."

Marci hesitated, then sat in a stuffed chair by the window.

"Wait here." Eve retrieved the red book from the greenhouse and returned to see that Marci hadn't so much as moved a muscle. She sat in a chair opposite the girl.

"If you don't mind, Marci, I will be direct. Is that okay?"

Marci looked at the roses. No response.

"Then we're agreed. Your problem, child, is that you're ugly only because you think you're ugly. You're ugly because you insist that you're ugly."

Marci glared at her. Started to stand. "This is—"

"Sit down!" Eve said.

Marci sat, more from shock than of her own choosing, Eve guessed.

"You've come all this way, and I intend to at least give this a whirl. Have you lost your mind, child? I'm talking about making you beautiful, and you're just going to walk out?"

"I'm not interested in inner beauty," Marci said. "I've heard enough speeches about inner—"

"I thought I made that clear. I'm not talking about inner anything. I'm talking about something you can see with your eyes." Eve set the book on the end table and crossed her legs. "Maybe I misjudged you after all. Maybe you're not the best candidate for the story."

"What story? You're really talking about physical beauty? You can't do that. No one can do that. What are you, a witch?"

•

12

"Yes, physical beauty. And it's not the power of devils that will change you. God forbid." Eve paused. "But I can promise you one thing, if it does change you—and it will if you let it—you'll never have any reason to hate yourself again. Any such thought will be the furthest from your mind, because you will love yourself, the new, beautiful you."

Marci glanced at the book, then up into Eve's eyes. "What story?"

*So strong and yet so very weak.* "Tea?" Eve asked.

"No thanks."

"Okay." Eve reached for the book and set it on her lap. "I'm going to tell you the story. You must listen very carefully to every word, because one of the characters will actually be you, and no one except you will know which one. I want you to find the character. Become that character. Embrace it. Her. Him. Whoever it is. Do you understand?"

"Then what?"

"Then we will see. But first you must agree to this."

"You're serious? What does this have to do with making me beautiful?"

"You think you're the first one to sit in that chair?"

"Did the others change?"

"All of them."

Despite her attempt to hide it, Marci's interest had grown. Her breathing sounded a little heavier. The morning was still and the scent of gardenia blossoms strong.

"If I have to."

"Have to what?" Eve asked.

"I'll pretend I'm one of the characters."

"You *are* one of them," Eve said. "No pretending here. Just figure out which one you are."

"Okay."

"Good. I want you to take a mental journey with me. I want you to go back with me to World War II. To a small village in Yugoslavia where a priest and his flock lived in complete peace. Women and children. No men, because they had been called off to war. Are you following me?"

"Yes."

"Good. Remember, you are there. You are one of the characters. I want you to figure out which one."

"I *know*."

"Good. It's a calm morning in the village. The grass in the valley is green and the sun is bright. Birds are chirping and children are laughing. There are fewer than a hundred there, all told. All women and children, except for Father Michael, who is standing on the steps of the church, watching the preparations for the celebration. It's Nadia's birthday, you see. She's turning thirteen. Do you have the scene?"

"Yes."

14

"Good. And from a hill above the village, five soldiers who've stumbled into this valley are watching. Can you see them?"

Marci nodded.

"On that day, hell collided with heaven, and it all started with the soldiers."

Marci's eyes had softened. She was listening. She was already entering the story.

Eve opened the book on her lap and read aloud.

# CHAPTER THREE

THE SOLDIERS stood unmoving on the hill's crest, leaning on battered rifles, five dark silhouettes against a white Bosnian sky, like a row of trees razed by the war. They stared down at the small village, oblivious to the sweat caked beneath their tattered army fatigues, unaware of the dirt streaking down their faces like long black claws.

Their condition wasn't unique. Any soldier who managed to survive the brutal fighting that ravaged Yugoslavia during its liberation from the Nazis looked the same. Or worse. A severed arm perhaps. Or bloody stumps below the waist. The country was strewn with dying wounded—testaments to Bosnia's routing of the enemy.

But the scene in the valley below them was unique. The village appeared untouched by the war. If a shell had landed anywhere near it during the years of bitter conflict, there was no sign of it now.

Several dozen homes with steep cedar shake roofs and white chimney smoke clustered neatly around the village center. Cobblestone paths ran like spokes between the homes and the large structure at the hub. There, with a sprawling courtyard, stood an ancient church with a belfry that reached to the sky like a finger pointing the way to God.

"What's the name of this village?" Karadzic asked no one in particular.

Janjic broke his stare at the village and looked at his commander. The man's lips had bent into a frown. He glanced at the others who were still captivated by this postcard-perfect scene below.

"I don't know," Molosov said to Janjic's right. "We're less than fifty clicks from Sarajevo. I grew up in Sarajevo."

"And what is your point?"

"My point is that I grew up in Sarajevo, and I don't remember this village."

Karadzic was a tall man, six foot two at least, and boxy above the waist. His bulky torso rested on spindly legs, like a bulldog born on stilts. His face was square and leathery, pitted by a collage of small scars, each marking another chapter in a violent past. Glassy gray eyes peered past thick, bushy eyebrows.

Janjic shifted on his feet and looked up-valley. What was left of the Partisan army waited a hard day's march north. But no one seemed eager to move. A bird's caw drifted through the air, followed by another. Two ravens circled lazily over the village.

"I don't remember seeing a church like this before. It looks wrong to me," Karadzic said.

A small tingle ran up Janjic's spine. Wrong? "We have a long march ahead of us, sir. We could make the regiment by nightfall if we leave now."

Karadzic ignored him entirely. "Puzup, have you seen an Orthodox church like this?"

Puzup blew smoke from his nose and drew deeply on his cigarette. "No, I guess I haven't."

"Molosov?"

"It's standing, if that's what you mean." He grinned. "It's been awhile since I've seen a church standing. Doesn't look Orthodox."

"If it isn't Orthodox, then what is it?"

"Not Jewish," Puzup said. "Isn't that right, Paul?"

"Not unless Jews have started putting crosses on their temples in my absence."

Puzup cackled in a high pitch, finding humor where apparently no one else did. Molosov reached over and slapped the younger soldier on the back of his head. Puzup's laugh stuck in his throat, and he grunted in protest. No one paid them any mind. Puzup clamped his lips around his cigarette. The tobacco crackled quietly in the stillness. The man absently picked at a bleeding scab on his right forearm.

Janjic spit to the side, anxious to rejoin the main army. "If we keep to the ridges, we should be able to maintain high ground and still meet the column by dark."

"It appears deserted," Molosov said, as if he had not heard Janjic.

"There's smoke. And there's a group in the courtyard," Paul said.

"Of course there's smoke. I'm not talking about smoke; I'm talking about people. You can't see if there's a group in the courtyard. We're two miles out."

"Look for movement. If you look—"

"Shut up," Karadzic snapped. "It's Franciscan." He shifted his Kalashnikov from one set of thick, gnarled fingers to the other.

A fleck of spittle rested on the commander's lower lip, and he made no attempt to remove it. Karadzic wouldn't know the difference between a Franciscan monastery and an Orthodox church if they stood side by side, Janjic thought. But that was beside the point. They all knew about Karadzic's hatred for the Franciscans.

"Our orders are to reach the column as soon as possible," Janjic said. "Not to scour the few standing churches for monks cowering in the corner. We have a war to finish, and it's not against them." He turned to view the town, surprised by his own insolence. *It is the war. I've lost my sensibilities.*

Smoke still rose from a dozen random chimneys; the ravens still circled. An eerie quiet hovered over the morning. He could feel the commander's gaze on his face—more than one man had died for less.

Molosov glanced at Janjic and then spoke softly to Karadzic. "Sir, Janjic is right—"

"Shut up! We're going down." Karadzic hefted his rifle and snatched it from the air cleanly. He faced Janjic. "We don't enlist women in this war, but you, Janjic, you are like a woman." He headed downhill.

One by one the soldiers stepped from the crest and strode for the peaceful village below. Janjic brought up the rear, swallowing uneasily. He had pushed it too far with the commander.

High above, the two ravens cawed again. It was the only sound besides the crunching of their boots.

FATHER MICHAEL saw the soldiers when they entered the cemetery at the edge of the village. Their small shapes emerged out of the green meadow like a row of tattered scarecrows. He pulled up at the top of the church's hewn stone steps, and a chill crept down his spine. For a moment the children's laughter about him waned.

*Dear God, protect us.* He prayed as he had a hundred times before, but he couldn't stop the tremors that took to his fingers.

The smell of hot baked bread wafted through his nostrils. A shrill giggle echoed through the courtyard; water gurgled from the natural spring to his left. Father Michael stood, stooped, and looked past the courtyard in which the children and women were celebrating Nadia's birthday, past the tall stone cross that marked the entrance to the graveyard, past the red rosebushes Claudis Flauta had so carefully planted about her home, to the lush hillside on the south.

To the four—no, five—to the five soldiers approaching.

He glanced around the courtyard—the children laughed and played. None of the others had seen the soldiers yet. High above, ravens cawed, and Michael looked up to see four of them circling.

*Father, protect your children.* A flutter of wings to his right caught his attention. He turned and watched a white dove settle for a landing on the vestibule's roof. The bird cocked its head and eyed him in small, jerky movements.

"Father Michael?" a child's voice said.

Michael turned to face Nadia, the birthday girl. She wore a pink dress reserved for special occasions. Her lips and nose were wide, and she had blotchy freckles on both cheeks. A homely girl even with the pretty pink dress. Some might even say ugly. Her mother, Ivena, was quite pretty; the coarse looks were from her father.

To make matters worse for the poor child, her left leg was two inches shorter than her right because of polio—a bad case when she was only three. Perhaps her handicap united her with Michael in ways the others could not understand. She with her short leg; he with

22

his hunched back.

Yet Nadia carried herself with a courage that defied her lack of physical beauty. At times Michael felt terribly sorry for the child, if for no other reason than that she didn't realize how her ugliness might handicap her in life. At other times his heart swelled with pride for her, for the way her love and joy shone with a brilliance that washed her skin clean of the slightest blemish.

He suppressed the urge to sweep her off her feet and swing her around in his arms. "Come unto me as little children," the Master had said. If only the whole world were filled with the innocence of children.

"Yes?"

NADIA LOOKED into Father Michael's eyes and saw the flash of pity before he spoke. It was more of a question than a statement, that look of his. More "Are you sure you're okay?" than "You look so lovely in your new dress."

None of them knew how well she could read their thoughts, perhaps because she'd long ago accepted the pity as a part of her life. Still, the realization that she limped and looked a bit plainer than most girls, regardless of what Mother told her, gnawed gently at her consciousness most of the time.

"Petrus says that since I'm thirteen now, all the boys will want to marry me. I told him that he's being a foolish boy, but he insists on running around making a silly game of it. Could you please tell him to stop?"

Petrus ran up, sneering. If any of the town's forty-three children was a bully, it was this ten-year-old know-nothing brat. Oh, he had his sweet side, Mother assured her. And Father Michael repeatedly said as much to the boy's mother, who was known to run about the village with her apron flying, leaving puffs of flour in her wake, shaking her rolling pin while calling for the runt to get his little rear end home.

"Nadia loves Milus! Nadia love Milus!" Petrus chanted and skipped by, looking back, daring her to take up chase.

"You're a misguided fledgling, Petrus," Nadia said, crossing her arms. "A silly little bird, squawking too much. Why don't you find your worms somewhere else?"

Petrus pulled up, flushing red. "Oh, you with all your fancy words! You're the one eating worms. With Milus. Nadia and Milus sitting in a tree, eating all the worms they can see!" He sang the verse again and ran off with a *whoop*, obviously delighted with his victory.

Nadia placed her hands on her hips and tapped the foot of her shorter leg with a disgusted sigh. "You see. Please stop him, Father."

"Of course, darling. But you know that he's just playing." Father Michael smiled and took a seat on the top step.

He looked over the courtyard, and Nadia followed his gaze. Of the village's seventy or so people, all but ten or twelve had come today for her birthday. Only the men were missing, called off to fight the Nazis. The old people sat in groups around the stone tables, grinning and chatting as they watched the children play a party game of balancing boiled eggs on spoons as they raced in a circle.

Nadia's mother, Ivena, directed the children with flapping hands, straining to be heard over their cries of delight. Three of the mothers busied themselves over a long table on which they had arranged pastries and the cake Ivena had fretted over for two days. It was perhaps the grandest cake Nadia had ever seen, a foot high, white with pink roses made from frosting.

All for her. All to cover up whatever pity they had for her and make her feel special.

Father Michael's gaze moved past the courtyard. Nadia looked up and saw a small band of soldiers approaching. The sight made her heart stop for a moment.

"Come here, Nadia."

Father Michael lifted an arm for her to sit by him, and she limped up the steps. She sat beside him, and he pulled her close.

He seemed nervous. The soldiers.

She put her arm around him, rubbing his humped back.

Father Michael swallowed and kissed the top of her head. "Don't mind Petrus. But he is right; one day the men will line up to marry such a pretty girl as you."

She ignored the comment and looked back at the soldiers who

were now in the graveyard, not a hundred yards off. They were Partisans, she saw with some relief. Partisans were probably friendly.

High above, birds cawed. Again Nadia followed the father's gaze as he looked up. Five ravens circled against the white sky. Michael looked to his right, to the vestibule roof. Nadia saw the lone dove staring on, clucking, with one eye peeled to the courtyard.

Father Michael looked back at the soldiers. "Nadia, go tell your mother to come."

Nadia hoped the soldiers wouldn't spoil her birthday party.

# CHAPTER FOUR

JANJIC JOVIC, the nineteen-year-old writer turned soldier, followed the others into the village, trudging with the same rhythmic cadence his marching had kept in the endless months leading up to this day. Just one foot after another. Ahead and to the right, Karadzic marched deliberately. The other three fanned out to his left.

Karadzic's war had less to do with defeating the Nazis than with restoring Serbia, and that included purging the land of anyone who wasn't a good Serb. Especially Franciscans.

Or so he said. They all knew that Karadzic killed good Serbs as easily as Franciscans. His own mother, for example, with a knife, he'd bragged, never mind that she was Serbian to the marrow. Though sure of few things, Janjic was certain the commander wasn't beyond trying to kill him one day. Janjic was a philosopher, a writer, not a killer, and the denser man despised him for it. He determined to follow Karadzic obediently regardless of the officer's folly; anything less could cost dearly.

Only when they were within a stone's throw of the village did Janjic study the scene with a careful eye. They approached from the south, through a graveyard holding fifty or sixty concrete crosses. So few graves. In most villages throughout Bosnia, one could expect to find hundreds if not thousands of fresh graves, pushing into lots never intended for the dead. They were evidence of a war gone mad.

But in this village, hidden here in this lush green valley, he counted fewer than ten plots that looked recent.

He studied the neat rows of houses—fewer than fifty—also unmarked by the war. The tall church spire rose high above the houses, adorned with a white cross, brilliant against the dull sky. The rest of the structure was cut from gray stone and elegantly carved like most churches. Small castles made for God.

None in the squad cared much for God—not even the Jew, Paul. But in Bosnia, religion had little to do with God. It had to do with who was right and who was wrong, not with who loved God. If you weren't Orthodox or at least a good Serb, you weren't right. If you were a Christian but not an Orthodox Christian, you weren't right. If you were Franciscan, you were most certainly not right. Janjic wasn't sure he disagreed with Karadzic on this point—

religious affiliation was more a defining line of this war than the Nazi occupation.

The Ustashe, Yugoslavia's version of the German Gestapo, had murdered hundreds of thousands of Serbs using techniques that horrified even the Nazis. Worse, they'd done it with the blessing of both the Catholic archbishop of Sarajevo and the Franciscans, neither of whom evidently understood the love of God. But then, *no* one in this war knew much about the love of God. It was a war absent of God, if indeed there even was such a being.

A child ran past the walls that surrounded the courtyard, out toward the tall cross, not fifty feet from them now. A boy, dressed in a white shirt and black shorts, with suspenders and a bow tie. The child slid to a halt, eyes popping.

Janjic smiled at the sight. The smell of hot bread filled his nostrils.

"Petrus! You come back here!"

A woman, presumably the boy's mother, ran for the boy, grabbed his arm, and yanked him back toward the churchyard. He struggled free and began marching in imitation of a soldier. *One, two! One, two!*

"Stop it, Petrus!" His mother caught his shirt and pulled him toward the courtyard.

Karadzic ignored the boy and kept his glassy gray eyes fixed ahead. Janjic was the last to enter the courtyard, following the others' clomping boots. Karadzic halted, and they pulled up behind him.

A priest stood on the ancient church steps, dressed in flowing black robes. Dark hair fell to his shoulders, and a beard extended several inches past his chin. He stood with a hunch in his shoulders.

A hunchback.

To his left, a flock of children sat on the steps in their mothers' arms, some of the mothers were smoothing their children's hair or stroking their cheeks. Smiling. All of them seemed to be smiling.

In all, sixty or seventy pairs of eyes stared at them.

"Welcome to Vares," the priest said, bowing politely.

They had interrupted a party of some kind. The children were dressed mostly in ties and dresses. A long table adorned with pastries and a cake sat untouched. The sight was surreal—a celebration of life in this countryside of death.

"What church is this?" Karadzic asked.

"Anglican," the priest said.

Karadzic glanced at his men, then faced the church. "I've never heard of this church."

A homely-looking girl in a pink dress suddenly stood from her mother's arms and walked awkwardly toward the table adorned with pastries. She hobbled.

Karadzic ignored her and twisted his fingers around the barrel of his rifle, tapping its butt on the stone. "Why is this church still standing?"

No one answered. Janjic watched the little girl place a golden brown pastry on a napkin.

"You can't speak?" Karadzic demanded. "Every church for a hundred kilometers is burned to the ground, but yours is untouched. And it makes me think that maybe you've been sleeping with the Ustashe."

"God has granted us favor," the priest said.

The commander paused. His lips twitched with a slight grin. A bead of sweat broke from the large man's forehead and ran down his flat cheek. "God has granted you favor? He's flown out of the sky and built an invisible shield over this valley to keep the bullets out, is that it?" His lips flattened. "God has allowed every Orthodox church in Yugoslavia to burn to the ground. And yet yours is standing."

Janjic watched the child limp toward a spring that gurgled in the corner and dip a mug into its waters. No one seemed to pay her any attention except the woman she had left on the steps, probably her mother.

Paul spoke quietly. "They're Anglican, not Franciscans or Catholics. I know Anglicans. Good Serbs."

"What does a Jew know about good Serbs?"

"I'm only telling you what I've heard," Paul said with a shrug.

The girl in the pink dress approached, carrying the mug of cold water in one hand and the pastry in the other. She stopped three feet from Karadzic and lifted the food to him. None of the villagers moved.

Karadzic ignored her. "And if your God is my God, why doesn't he protect my church? The Orthodox church?"

The priest smiled gently, still staring without blinking, hunched over on the steps.

"I'm asking you a question, Priest," Karadzic said.

"I can't speak for God," the priest said. "Perhaps you should ask him. We're God-loving people with no quarrel. But I cannot speak for God on all matters."

The small girl lifted the pastry and water higher. Karadzic's eyes took on that menacing stare Janjic had seen so many times before.

Janjic moved on impulse. He stepped up to the girl and smiled. "You're very kind," he said. "Only a good Serb would offer bread and water to a tired and hungry Partisan soldier." He reached for the pastry and took it. "Thank you."

A dozen children scrambled from the stairs and ran to the table, arguing about who was to be first. They quickly gathered up food to follow the young girl's example and then rushed for the soldiers, pastries in hand. Janjic was struck by their innocence. This was just another game to them. The sudden turn of events had effectively silenced Karadzic, but Janjic couldn't look at the commander. If Molosov and the others didn't follow his cue, there would be a price to pay later—this he knew with certainty.

"My name's Nadia," the young girl said, looking up at Janjic. "It's my birthday today. I'm thirteen years old."

Ordinarily Janjic would have answered the girl—told her what a brave thirteen-year-old she was, but today his mind was on his comrades. Several children now swarmed around Paul and Puzup, and Janjic saw with relief that they were accepting the pastries. With smiles in fact.

"We could use the food, sir," Molosov said.

Karadzic snatched up his hand to silence the second in command. Nadia held the cup in her hand toward him. Once again every eye turned to the commander, begging him to show some mercy. Karadzic suddenly scowled and slapped the cup aside. It clattered to the stone in a shower of water. The children froze.

Karadzic brushed angrily past Nadia. She backpedaled and fell to her bottom. The commander stormed over to the birthday table and kicked his boot against the leading edge. The entire birthday display rose into the air and crashed onto the ground.

Nadia scrambled to her feet and limped toward her mother, who drew her in. The other children scampered for the steps.

Karadzic turned to them, his face red. "Now do I have your attention?"

# CHAPTER FIVE

EVE PAUSED and closed her eyes. She could hear the commander's voice as though he were still alive, as alive as the day she had watched him with the rest.

She pursed her lips angrily, mimicking him. "Now do I have your attention?"

For years she told herself that they should have made the children leave then. Run back to the houses. But they hadn't. More recently she discovered the reason for that.

Reliving that day was never pleasant, but always it brought her an uncanny strength and a deep-seated peace. And more important, *not* to remember—indeed, not to participate again and again—would make a mockery of it. "Take this in remembrance of me," Christ had said. Participate in the suffering of Christ, Paul had said.

And yet so many Americans turned forgetting into a kind of

spiritual badge, refusing to memorialize suffering for fear they might catch it like a disease. Indeed, they stripped Christ of his dignity by ignoring the brutality of his death. The choice was no different than turning away from a puffy-faced leper in horror. The epitome of rejection.

How many had closed this book here and returned to their knitting in a huff? Perhaps to knit nice soft crosses for their grand-children.

It occurred to Eve that every muscle in her body had tensed.

She opened her eyes. Marci sat with a fixed stare.

"I'm sorry. Where were we?" She cleared her throat. "That's right, 'Do I have your attention?'"

"I'm not sure I like this story," Marci said. "Something's going to happen."

"It's not your business to like this story. It's your business to find out who you are in the story. And you're right. Something *is* going to happen, and it's going to happen to you if you'll let it. There is a power in this story!"

"It's just a story. Nothing magical or—"

"*Not* just a story! And who said anything about magic?" Eve said. "This is far more powerful than any magic. When you know who you are in the story, it will begin."

Marci's eyes grew slightly rounder. If the girl only knew.

Eve lifted the book and read.

"NOW DO I have your attention?"

Father Michael's heart seemed to stick midstroke. He mumbled his prayer now, loudly enough for the women nearest him to hear.

"Protect your children, Father."

The leader was possessed of the devil. Michael had known so from the moment the big man had entered the courtyard. *Yea, though I walk through the valley of the shadow of death, I will fear no evil.*

He barely heard the flutter of wings to his right. The dove had taken flight. The commander glared at him. *Now do I have your attention?*

The dove's wings beat through the air. *Yes, you have my attention, Commander. You had my attention before you began this insanity.* But he did not say it because the dove had stopped above him and was flapping noisily. The commander's eyes rose to the bird. Michael leaned back to compensate for his humped back and looked up.

In that moment, the world fell to a silent slow motion.

Michael could see the commander standing, legs spread. Above him, the white dove swept gracefully at the air, fanning a slight wind to him, like an angel breathing five feet above his head.

The breath moved through his hair, through his beard, cool at first, and then suddenly warm. High above the dove, a hole appeared in the clouds, allowing the sun to send its rays of warmth. Michael could see that the ravens still circled, more of them now—seven or eight.

This he saw in that first glance, as the world slowed to a crawl. Then he felt the music on the wind. At least that was how he thought of it, because the music didn't sound in his ears, but in his mind and in his chest.

Though only a few notes, they spread an uncanny warmth. A whisper that seemed to say, "My beloved."

Just that. Just, *My beloved*. The warmth suddenly rushed through him like water, past his loins, right down to the soles of his feet.

Father Michael gasped.

The dove took flight.

A chill of delight rippled up his back. Goodness! Nothing even remotely similar had happened to him in all of his years. *My beloved*. Like the anointing of Jesus at his baptism. *This is my beloved Son, in whom I am well pleased.*

He'd always taught that Christ's power is as real for the believer today as it was two thousand years earlier.

Now Michael had heard these words of love. *My beloved!* God was going to protect them.

It occurred to him that he was still bent back awkwardly and that his mouth had fallen open, like a man who'd been shot. He clamped it shut and jerked forward.

The rest hadn't heard the voice. Their eyes were on him, not on the dove, which had landed on the nearest roof—Sister Flauta's house, surrounded by those red rosebushes. The flowers' scent, thick and sweet, reached up into his sinuses. Which was odd. He should be fighting a panic just now, terrified of these men with guns. Instead his mind was taking time to smell Sister Flauta's rose-bushes. And pausing to hear the watery gurgle of the spring to his left.

A dumb grin lifted the corners of his mouth. He knew it was dumb because he had no business facing this monster before him wearing a snappy little grin. But he could hardly control it, and he quickly lifted a hand to cover his mouth. He supposed the gesture must look like a child hiding a giggle. It would infuriate the man.

And so it did.

"Wipe that idiotic grin off your face!"

The commander strode toward him. Except for the ravens caw-ing overhead and the spring's insistent gurgle, Father Michael could only hear his own heart, pounding like a boot against a hollow drum. His head still buzzed from the dove's words, but another thought slowly took form in his mind. It was the realization that he'd heard the music for a reason. It wasn't every day, or even every year, that heaven reached down so deliberately to a man.

Karadzic stopped and glared at the women and children. "So. You claim to be people of faith?"

He asked as if he expected an answer. Ivena looked at Father

Michael.

"Are you all mutes?" Karadzic demanded, red faced.

Still no one spoke.

Karadzic planted his legs far apart. "No. I don't think you *are* people of faith. I think that your God has abandoned you, perhaps when you and your murdering priests burned the Orthodox church in Glina after stuffing a thousand women and children into it."

Karadzic's lips twisted around the words. "Perhaps the smell of their charred bodies rose to the heavens and sent your God to hell."

"It was a horrible massacre," Father Michael heard himself say. "But it wasn't us, my friend. We abhor the brutality of the Ustashe. No God-fearing man could possibly take the life of another with such cruelty."

"I shot a man in the knees just a week ago before killing him. It was quite brutal. Are you saying that *I* am not a God-fearing man?"

"I believe that God loves all men, Commander. Me no more than you."

"Shut up! You sit back in your fancy church, singing pretty songs of love, while your men roam the countryside seeking a Serb to cut open."

"If you were to search the battlefields, you would find our men stitching up the wounds of soldiers, not killing them."

Karadzic squinted briefly at the claim. For a moment he just stared. He suddenly smiled, but it wasn't a kind smile.

"Then surely true faith can be proven." He spun to one of the soldiers. "Molosov, bring me one of the crosses from the graveyard."

The soldier looked at his commander with a raised brow.

"Are you deaf? Bring me a gravestone."

"They're in the ground, sir."

"Then pull it *out* of the ground!"

"Yes, sir." Molosov jogged across the courtyard and into the adjacent cemetery.

Father Michael watched the soldier kick at the nearest headstone, a cross like all the others, two feet in height, made of concrete. He knew the name of the deceased well. It was that of old man Haris Zecavic, planted in the ground over twenty years ago.

"What's the teaching of your Christ?"

Michael looked back at Karadzic, who still wore a twisted grin.

"Hmm? Carry your cross?" Karadzic said. "Isn't that what your God commanded you to do? 'Pick up your cross and follow me'?"

"Yes."

Molosov hauled the cross he'd freed into the courtyard. The villagers watched, stunned.

Karadzic gestured at them with his rifle. "Exactly. As you see, I'm not as stupid in matters of faith as you think. My own mother was a devout Christian. Then again, she was also a whore, which is why I know that not all Christians are necessarily right in the head."

The soldier dropped the stone at Karadzic's feet. It landed with a loud *thunk* and toppled flat. One of the women made a squeaking sound—Marie Zecavic, the old man's thirty-year-old daughter, mourning the destruction of her father's grave, possibly. The commander glanced at Marie.

"We're in luck today," Karadzic said, keeping his eyes on Marie. "Today we actually have a cross for you to bear. We will give you an opportunity to prove your faith. Come here."

Marie had a knuckle in her mouth, biting off her cry. She looked up with fear-fired eyes.

"Yes, you. Come here, please."

Father Michael took a step toward the commander. "Please—"

"Stay!"

Michael stopped. Fingers of dread tickled his spine. He nodded and tried to smile with warmth.

Marie stepped hesitantly toward the commander.

"Put the cross on her back," Karadzic said.

Father Michael stepped forward, instinctively raising his right hand in protest.

Karadzic whirled to him, lips twisted. "Stay!" His voice thundered across the courtyard.

Molosov bent for the cross, which could not weigh less than thirty kilos. Marie's face wrinkled in fear. Tears streaked silently down her cheeks.

Karadzic sneered. "Don't cry, child. You're simply going to carry a cross for your Christ. It's a noble thing, isn't it?"

He nodded, and his man hoisted the gravestone to Marie's back. Her body began to tremble, and Michael felt his heart expand.

"Don't just stand there, woman; hold it!" Karadzic snapped.

Marie leaned tentatively forward and reached back for the stone. Molosov released his grip. Her back sagged momentarily, and she staggered forward with one foot before steadying herself.

"Good. You see, it's not so bad." Karadzic stood back, pleased with himself. He turned to Father Michael. "Not so bad at all. But I tell you, Priest—if she drops the cross, then we will have a problem."

Michael's heart accelerated. Heat surged up his neck and flared around his ears. *Oh God, give us strength!*

"Yes, of course. If she drops the cross, it will mean that you are an impostor and that your church is unholy. We will be forced to remove some of your skin with a beating." The commander's twisted smile broadened.

Father Michael looked at Marie and tried to still his thumping heart. He nodded, mustering reserves of courage. "Don't be afraid, Marie. God's love will save us."

Karadzic stepped forward and swung his hand. A loud crack echoed from the walls, and Michael's head snapped back. The blow brought stinging tears to his eyes and blood to his mouth. He looked up at Sister Flauta's roof; the dove still perched on the peak, tilting its head to view the scene below. *Peace, my son.* Had he really heard that music? Yes. Yes, he had. God had actually spoken to him. God would protect them.

*Father, spare us. I beg you, spare us!*

"March, woman!" Karadzic pointed toward the far end of the courtyard. Marie stepped forward. The children looked on with bulging eyes. Stifled cries rippled through the courtyard.

They watched her heave the burden across the concrete, her feet straining with bulging veins at each footfall. Marie wasn't the strongest of them. *Oh God, why couldn't it have been another—Ivena, or even one of the older boys. But Marie? She will stumble at any moment!*

Michael could not hold his tongue. "Why do you test her? It's me—"

*Smack!*

The hand landed flat and hard enough to send him reeling back a step this time. A balloon of pain spread from his right cheek.

"Next time it'll be the stock of a rifle," the commander said.

Marie reached the far wall and turned back. She staggered by, searching Father Michael's eyes for help. Everyone watched her quietly, first one way and then the other, bent under the load, eyes darting in fear, slogging back and forth. Most of the soldiers seemed amused. They had undoubtedly seen atrocities that made this seem like a game in comparison. *Go on, prove your faith in Christ. Follow his teaching. Carry this cross. And if you drop it before we tire of watching, we will beat your priest to a bloody pulp.*

Michael prayed. *Father, I beg you. I truly beg you to spare us. I beg you!*

# CHAPTER SIX

IT WAS Nadia who refused to stay silent.

The homely birthday girl with her pigtails and her yellow hair clips stood, limped down the steps, and faced the soldiers, arms dangling by her sides. Father Michael swallowed. *Father, please!* He could not speak it, but his heart cried it out. *Please, Father!*

"Nadia!" Ivena whispered harshly.

But Nadia didn't even look her mother's way. Her voice carried across the courtyard clear and soft and sweet. "Father Michael has told us that people filled with Christ's love do not hurt other people. Why are you hurting Marie? She's done nothing wrong."

In that moment, Father Michael wished he had not taught them so well.

Karadzic looked at her, his gray eyes wide, his mouth slightly agape, obviously stunned.

"Nadia!" Ivena called out in a hushed cry. "Sit down!"

"Shut up!" Karadzic came to life. He stormed toward the girl, livid and red. "Shut up, shut up!" He shook his rifle at her. "Sit down, you ugly little runt!"

Nadia sat.

Karadzic stalked back and forth before the steps, his knuckles white on his gun, his lips trembling.

"You feel bad for your pitiful Marie, is that it? Because she's carrying this tiny cross on her back?"

He stopped in front of a group of three women huddling on the stairs and leaned toward them. "What is happening to Marie is nothing! Say it! Nothing!"

No one spoke.

Karadzic suddenly flipped his rifle to his shoulder and peered down its barrel at Sister Flauta. "Say it!"

A hard knot lodged in Father Michael's throat. His vision blurred with tears. This could not be happening! They were a peaceful, loving people who served a risen God. *Father, do not abandon us! Do not! Do not!*

The commander cocked the rifle to the sky with his right hand. His lips pressed white. "To the graveyard, then! All of you! All the women."

They only stared at him, unbelieving.

He shoved a thick, dirty finger toward the large cross at the cemetery's entrance and fired into the air. "Go!"

They went. Like a flock of geese, pattering down the steps and across the courtyard, some whimpering, others setting their jaws firm. Marie kept slogging across the stone yard. She was slowing, Michael thought.

The commander turned to his men. "Load a cross on every woman and bring them back."

The thin soldier with bright hazel eyes stepped forward in protest. "Sir—"

"Shut up!"

The soldiers jogged for the graveyard. Father Michael's vision swam. *Father, you are abandoning us! They are playing with your children!*

Several children moved close to him, tugging at his robe, embracing his leg. Blurred forms in uniform kicked at the headstone crosses and hoisted them to the backs of the women. They staggered back to the courtyard, bearing their heavy loads. It was impossible!

Father Michael watched his flock reduced to animals, bending under the weight of concrete crosses. He clenched his teeth. These were women, like Mary and Martha, with tender hearts full of love. Sweet, sweet women, who'd toiled in childbirth and nursed their babies through cold winters. He should rush the commander and smash his head against the rock! He should protect his sheep!

In his peripheral vision, Michael saw the dove clucking on the roofline, stepping from one foot to the other. The comforting words seemed distant now, so very abstract. *Peace, my son.* But this was not peace! This was barbarism!

The twisted smile found Karadzic's quivering lips again. "March," he ordered. "March, you pathetic slugs! We'll see how you like Christ's cross. And the first one to drop the cross will be beaten with the father!"

They walked with Marie, twenty-three of them, bowed under their loads, silent except for heavy breathing and padding feet, staggering.

Every bone in Michael's body screamed in protest now. *Stop this! Stop this immediately! It's insanity! Take me, you spineless cowards! I will carry their crosses. I will carry all of their crosses. You may bury me under their crosses if you wish, but leave these dear women alone! For the love of God!* His whole body trembled as the words rushed through his head.

But they did not reach his lips. They could not, because his throat had seized shut in anguish. And in any case, the insane commander might very well take the butt of his gun to one of them if he spoke.

A child whimpered at Michael's knee. He bit his lower lip, closed his eyes, and rested a hand on the boy's head. *Father, please.* His bones shook with the inward groan. Tears spilled down his cheeks now, and he felt one land on his hand, wet and warm. His humped shoulders begged to shake—to sob—to cry out for relief, but he refused to disintegrate before all of them. He was their shepherd, for heaven's sake! He was not one of the women or one of the children; he was a man. God's chosen vessel for this little village in a land savaged by war.

He breathed deeply and closed his eyes. *Dearest Jesus . . . My dearest Jesus . . .*

The world changed then, for the second time that day. A brilliant flash ignited in his mind, as if someone had taken a picture with one of those bulbs that popped and burned out. Father Michael's body jerked, and he snapped his eyes open. He might have gasped—he wasn't sure, because this world, with all of its soldiers and trudging women, was too distant to judge accurately.

In its place stretched a white horizon flooded with streaming light. And music.

Faint but clear. Long, pure notes, the same as he'd heard earlier. *My beloved.* A song of love.

Michael shifted his gaze to the horizon and squinted. The landscape was endless and flat like a sprawling desert, but covered with white flowers. From the distant horizon, the light streamed above the ground toward him.

A tiny wedge of alarm struck Michael. He was alone in this white field. Except for the light, of course. The light and the music.

He could suddenly hear more in the music. At first he thought it might be the spring bubbling near the courtyard. But it wasn't water.

51

It was a sound made by a child. It was a child's laughter, distant, but rushing toward him from that far horizon, carried on the swelling notes of music.

Gooseflesh rippled over Michael's skin. He suddenly felt as though he might be floating, swept off his feet by a deep note that resounded in his bones.

The music grew, and with it the children's laughter. High peals of laughter and giggles, not from one child, but from a hundred children. Maybe a thousand children, or a million, swirling around him now from every direction. Laughter of delight, as though from a small boy being mercilessly tickled by his father. Then reprieves followed by sighs of contentment as others took up the laughing.

Michael could not help the giggle that bubbled in his own chest and slipped out in short bursts. The sound was thoroughly intoxicating. But where were the children?

A single melody reached through the music. A man's voice, pure and clear, with the power to melt whatever it touched. Michael stared out at the field where the sound came from.

A man was walking his way, a shimmering figure, still only an inch tall on the horizon. The voice was his. He hummed a simple melody, but it flowed over Michael with intoxicating power. The melody started low and rose through the scale and then paused. Immediately the children's laughter swelled, responding directly to the man's song. He began again, and the giggles quieted a little and then swelled at the end of this simple refrain. It was like a game.

Michael couldn't hold back his own laughter. *Oh my God, what is happening to me? I'm losing my mind.* Who was this minstrel walking toward him? And what kind of song was this that made him want to fly with all those children he could not see?

Michael lifted his head and searched the skies. *Come out, come out wherever you are, my children.* Were they his children? He had no children.

But now he craved them. *These* children, laughing hysterically around him. He wanted these children—to hold them, to kiss them, to run his fingers through their hair and roll on the ground, laughing with them. To sing this song to them. *Come out, my dear . . .*

The flashbulb ignited again. *Pop!*

The laughter evaporated. The song was gone.

It took only a moment for Father Michael to register the simple, undeniable fact that he was once again standing on the steps of his church, facing a courtyard filled with women who slumped under heavy crosses over cold, flat concrete. His mouth lay open, and he seemed to have forgotten how to use the muscles in his jaw.

The soldiers stood against the far wall, smirking at the women, except for the tall, skinny man. He seemed awkward in his role. The commander looked on with a glint in his eyes. And then Michael realized that they had not seen his awkward display of laughter.

Above them the dove perched on Sister Flauta's roof, still eyeing the scene below. To Michael's right, the elderly still sat, as though dead in their seats, unbelieving of this nightmare unfolding before them. And at his fingertips, a head of hair. He quickly closed his mouth and looked down. Children. His children.

But these were not laughing. These were seated, or standing against his legs, some staring quietly at their mothers, others whimpering. Nadia, the birthday girl, sat stoically on the end, her jaw clenched, her hands on her knees.

When Father Michael looked up, his eyes met Ivena's as she trudged under her cross. They were bright and sorrowful at once. She seemed to understand something, but he could not know what. Perhaps she, too, had heard the song. Either way, he smiled, somehow less afraid than he had been just a minute ago.

Because he knew something now.

He knew there were two worlds in motion here.

He knew that behind the skin of this world, there was another. And in that world a man was singing, and the children were laughing.

# CHAPTER SEVEN

JANJIC LOOKED at the women shuffling across the courtyard and bit back his growing anger with this demented game of Karadzic's.

He'd dutifully kicked over three gravestones and hefted them onto the backs of terrified women. One of them was the birthday girl's mother. Ivena, he heard someone call her.

Janjic could see that she'd taken care to dress for her daughter's special day. Imitation pearls hung around her neck. She wore her hair in a meticulous bun, and the dress she'd chosen was neatly pressed; a light pink dress with tiny yellow flowers so that she matched her daughter.

How long had they planned for this party? A week? A month? The thought brought nausea to his gut. These souls were innocent of anything deserving such humiliation. There was something obscene about forcing mothers to lug the ungainly religious symbols while their children looked on.

Ivena could easily be his own mother, holding him after his father's death ten years earlier. Mother, dear Mother—Father's death nearly killed her as well. At ten, Janjic became the man of the house. It was a tall calling. His mother died three days after his eighteenth birthday, leaving him with nothing but the war to join.

The women's dresses were darkened with sweat now, their faces wrinkled with pain, their eyes casting furtive glances at their frightened children on the steps. Still they plodded, back and forth like old mules. Yes, it was obscene.

But then the whole war was obscene.

The priest stood still in his long black robe, hunched over. A dumb look of wonder had captured his face for a moment, then passed. Perhaps he had already fallen into the abyss, watching the women slog their way past him. *Pray to your God, Priest. Tell him to stop this madness before one of your women drops her cross. We have a march to make.*

From his right the sound came, like the sickening crunch of bones, jerking Janjic out of his reverie. He turned his head. One of the women was on her knees, trembling, her hands limp on the ground, her face knotted in distress around clenched eyes.

Marie had dropped her cross.

Movement in the courtyard froze. As one, the women stopped in their tracks. Every eye stared at the cement cross lying facedown on the concrete beside the woman. Karadzic's face lit up as though the contact of cross with ground completed a circuit that flooded his skull with electricity. A quiver had taken to his lower lip.

Janjic swallowed. The commander snorted once and took three long steps toward Marie. The priest also took a step toward his fallen sheep but stopped when Karadzic spun back to him.

"When your backs are up against the wall, you can no more follow the teachings of Christ than any of us. Perhaps that's why the Jews butchered the man, eh, Paul? Maybe his teachings really were the rantings of a lunatic, impossible for any sane man."

The priest's head snapped up. "It's *God* you speak of!"

Karadzic turned slowly to him. "*God,* you say? The Jews killed *God* on a cross, then? You may not be a Franciscan, but you're as stupid."

Father Michael's face flushed red. His eyes shone in shock. "It was for *love* that Christ walked to his death," he said.

Janjic shifted on his feet and felt his pulse quicken. The man of cloth had found his backbone.

"Christ was a fool. Now he's a dead fool," Karadzic said. The words echoed through the courtyard. He paced before Father Michael, his face frozen in a frown.

"Christ lives. He is not dead," the priest said.

"Then let him save you."

The burly commander glared at the priest, who stood tall, soaking in the insults for his God. The sight unnerved Janjic.

Father Michael drew a deep breath. "Christ lives in me, sir. His spirit rages through my body. I feel it now. I can hear it. The only reason that you can't is because your eyes and ears are clogged by this world. But there's another world at work here. It's Christ's kingdom, and it bristles with his power."

Karadzic took a step back, blinking at the priest's audacity. He suddenly ran for Marie, who was still crumpled on the cement. A dull thump resounded with each boot-fall. In seven long strides he reached her. He swung his rifle like a bat, slamming the wooden butt down on the woman's shoulder. She grunted and fell to her belly.

Sharp gasps filled the air. Karadzic poised his rifle for another blow and twisted to face the priest. "You say you have power? Show me, then!" He landed another blow, and the woman moaned.

"Please!" The priest took two steps forward and fell to his knees, his face wrinkled with grief. Tears streamed from his eyes. "Please, it's me you said you would beat!" He clasped his hands together as if in prayer. "Leave her, I beg you. She's innocent."

The rifle butt landed twice on the woman's head, and her body relaxed. Several children began to cry; a chorus of women groaned in shock, still bent under their own heavy loads. The sound grated on Janjic's ears.

"Please . . . please," Father Michael begged.

"Shut up! Janjic, beat him!"

Janjic barely heard the words. His eyes were fixed on the priest.

"Janjic! Beat him." Karadzic pointed with an extended arm. "Ten blows!"

Janjic turned to the commander, still not fully grasping the order. This wasn't his quarrel. It was Karadzic's game. "Beat him? Me? I—"

"You question me?" The commander took a threatening step toward Janjic. "You'll do as I say. Now take your rifle and lay it across this traitor's back, or I'll have *you* shot!"

Janjic felt his mouth open.

"Now!"

Two emotions crashed through Janjic's chest. The first was simple revulsion at the prospect of swinging a fifteen-pound rifle at this priest's deformed back. The second was fear at the realization that he felt any revulsion at all. He was a soldier who'd sworn to follow orders. And he had always followed orders. It was his only way to survive the war. But this . . .

He swallowed and took a step toward the figure, bent now in an attitude of prayer. The children stared at him—thirty sets of round, white-rimmed eyes, swimming in tears, all crying a single question. *Why?*

He glanced at Karadzic's red face. The commander's neck bulged like a bullfrog's, and his eyes bored into Janjic. *Because he told me to,* Janjic answered. *Because this man is my superior, and he told me to.*

Janjic raised his rifle and stared at the man's hunched back. It was trembling now, he saw. A hard blow might break that back. A knot rose to Janjic's throat. How could he do this? It was lunacy! He lowered the rifle, his mind scrambling for reason.

"Sir, should I make him stand?"

"Should you *what*?"

"Should I make him stand? I could handle the rifle better if he would stand. It would give me a greater attitude to target—"

"Make him stand, then!"

"Yes, sir. I just thought—"

"Move!"

"Yes, sir."

A slight quiver had taken to Janjic's hands. His arms ached under the rifle's weight. He nudged the kneeling priest with his boot.

"Stand, please."

The priest stood slowly and turned to face him. He cast a side glance to the crumpled form near the commander. His tears were for the woman, Janjic realized. There was no fear in his eyes, only remorse over the abuse of one of his own.

He couldn't strike this man! It would be the death of his own soul to do so!

"Beat him!"

Janjic flinched.

"Turn, please," he instructed.

The father turned sideways.

Janjic had no choice. At least that was what he told himself as he drew his rifle back. *It's an order. This is a war. I swore to obey all orders. It's an order. I'm a soldier at war. I have an obligation.*

He swung the rifle by the barrel, aiming for the man's lower back. The sound of sliced air preceded a fleshy *thump* and a grunt from the priest. The man staggered forward and barely caught his fall.

Heat flared up Janjic's back, tingling at the base of his head. Nausea swept through his gut.

The father stood straight again. He looked strong enough, but Janjic knew he might very well have lost a kidney to that blow. A tear stung the corner of his eye. Good God, he was going to *cry*! Janjic panicked.

*I'm a soldier, for the love of country! I'm a Partisan! I'm not a coward!*

He swung again, with fury this time. The blow went wild and struck the priest on his shoulder. Something gave way with a loud snap—the butt of his rifle. Janjic pulled the gun back, surprised that he could break the wood stock so easily.

But the rifle was not broken.

He jerked his eyes to the priest's shoulder. It hung limp. Janjic felt the blood drain from his head. He saw Father Michael's face then. The priest was expressionless, as if he'd lost consciousness while on his feet.

Janjic lost his sensibilities then. He landed a blow as much to silence the voices screaming through his brain as to carry out his orders. He struck again, like a man possessed with the devil, frantic to club the black form before him into silence. He was not aware of the loud moan that broke from his throat until he'd landed six of the blows. His seventh missed, not because he had lost his aim, but because the priest had fallen.

Janjic spun, carried by the swing. The world came back to him then. His comrades standing by the wall, eyes wide with astonishment; the women still bent under concrete crosses; the children whimpering and crying and burying their heads in each other's bosoms.

The priest knelt on the concrete, heaving, still expressionless. Blood began to pool on the ground below his face. Some bones had shattered there.

Janjic felt the rifle slip from his hands. It clattered to the concrete.

"Finish it!" Karadzic's voice echoed in the back of Janjic's head, but he did not consider the matter. His legs were shaking, and he backed unsteadily from the black form huddled at his feet.

To his right, boots thudded on the concrete and Janjic turned just in time to see his commander rushing at him with a raised rifle. He instinctively threw his arms up to cover his face. But the blows did not come. At least not to him.

They landed with a sickening finality on the priest's back. Three blows in quick succession accompanied by another snap. The thought that one of the women may have stepped on a twig stuttered through Janjic's mind. But he knew that the snap had come from the father's ribs. He staggered back to the wall and crashed against it.

"You will pay for this, Janjic," Molosov muttered.

Janjic's mind reeled, desperate to correct his spinning world. *Get ahold of yourself, Janjic! You're a soldier! Yes, indeed, a soldier who defied his superior's orders. What kind of madness has come over you?*

He straightened. His comrades were turned from him, watching Karadzic yank the priest to his feet. Janjic looked at the soldiers and saw that a line of sweat ran down the Jew's cheek. Puzup blinked repeatedly.

The priest suddenly gasped. *Uhhh!* The sound echoed in the silence.

Karadzic hardly seemed to notice the odd sound. "March!" he thundered. "The next one to drop a cross will receive twenty blows with the priest. We'll see what kind of faith he has taught you."

The women tottered, gaping, sagging.

The commander gripped his hands into fists. Cords of muscle stood out on his neck. "Maaarch!"

They marched.

# CHAPTER EIGHT

EVE SLOWLY lowered the book with a quiver in her hands. After so many years, the pain had not lessened. She leaned back and drew a deep breath.

She leapt from her chair. "March!" she mimicked, and she strutted across the floor, the book flapping in her right hand. "Maaarch! One, two. One, two." She did it with indignation and fury, and she did it hardly thinking what she was doing.

She was aware of Marci to her right and then her left as she turned, but emotion caught her up too quickly for her to bother with modesty. She had entered the story herself, precisely as she had asked Marci to. If the girl had any real sense of it yet, she might jump up and join Eve.

"Maaarch!"

MARCI WATCHED Eve march across the living room. She felt an odd compunction to jump up and join her. She saw Eve as defiant, mocking Karadzic for being such a pig. Eve was marching because she was actually in the story, right here, right now.

And so was Marci, wasn't she? She was present, seeing glimpses of what Father Michael was seeing. What did it mean? And who was she? Maybe all of them, but no, Eve had said one character.

One thing was certain, there were two worlds in the story. A brutal, ugly world, and a lovely, beautiful world. Somehow Father Michael was in both. And somehow she was in two worlds too.

"So . . . what happens?" Marci asked.

Eve stopped marching and looked at her, startled. "What?"

"I'm sorry. Um . . . are we going to finish?"

"Yes." Eve slipped back into her chair. "Yes, I'm sorry. I got a bit carried . . . Where was I?"

"You were marching."

"I was marching. And you were starting to see." She peeked at Marci, lifted an eyebrow, then lowered her eyes to the page.


FATHER MICHAEL remembered arguing with the commander; remembered Karadzic's rifle butt smashing down on Sister Marie's skull; remembered the other soldier, the skinny one, making him stand and then raising the rifle to strike him. He even remembered closing his eyes against that first blow to his kidneys. But that blow ignited the strobe in his mind.

*Poof!*

The courtyard vanished in a flash of light.

The white desert crashed into his world. Fingers of light streaked from the horizon. The ground was covered with the white flowers. And the music!

Oh, the music. The children's laughter rode the skies, playing off the man's song. His volume had grown, intensified, compelling Michael to join in the laughter. The same simple tune, but now others seemed to have joined in to form a chorus. Or maybe it just sounded like a chorus but was really just laughter.

*Sing, O son of Zion; Shout, O child of mine;*
*Rejoice with all your heart and soul and mind.*

Michael was vaguely aware of a crashing on the edge of his world. It was as if he lived in a Christmas ornament, and a child had taken a stick to it. But it wasn't a stick; he knew that. It wasn't a child either. It was the soldier with a rifle beating his bones.

He heard a loud snap. *I've got to hurry up before the roof caves in about me! I've got to hurry! My bones are breaking.*

Hurry? Hurry where?

Hurry to meet this man. Hurry to find the children, of course.

Problem was, he still couldn't see them. He could hear them, all right. Their laughter rippled over the field in long, uncontrolled strings that forced a smile to his mouth.

The figure was still far away, a foot high on the horizon now, walking straight toward Michael, singing his incredible song. He would have expected music to reach him through his ears, but this song didn't bother with the detour. It seemed to reach right through his chest and squeeze his heart. Love and hope and sorrow and laughter all rolled up in one.

He opened his mouth without thinking and sang a couple of the words. *O child of mine* . . . A silly grin spread his cheeks. What did he think he was doing? But he felt a growing desperation to sing with the man, to match the chorus with his own. *La da da, da la!* Mozart! An angel with the purest melody known to man. To God!

And he wanted to laugh! He almost did. He almost threw back his head and cackled. His chest felt as though it might explode with the desire. But he could not see the children. And that stick was making an awful racket about his bones.

Without ceremony, the world with all of its color and light and music was jerked from him. He was back in the village.

He heard himself gasp. *Uhhh!* It was like having a bucket of cold water thrown at him while taking a warm shower. He was standing now, facing Marie's fallen body. The spring gurgled on as if nothing at all had happened. The women were frozen in place. The children were crying.

And pain was spreading through his flesh like leaking acid.

*Oh God. What is happening? What are you doing to your children?*

His shoulder did not feel right. Neither did his cheek.

He wanted to be back in the laughing world with the children. Marie stirred on the ground. The commander was screaming, and now the women started to move, like ghosts in a dream.

*No.* The colors of Father Michael's world brightened. *No, I do not belong with the laughing children. I belong here with my own children. These whom God has given me charge over. They need me.*

But he didn't know what he should do. He wasn't even sure he could talk. So he prayed. He cried out to God to save them from this wicked man.

THE COURTYARD had become a wasteland, Janjic thought. A wasteland filled with frozen guards and whimpering children and moaning women. The ravens soared in an unbroken circle now, a dozen strong. A lone dove watched the scene from its perch on the house to his right.

Janjic swallowed, thinking that he might cry. But he would swallow his tongue before he allowed tears. He had humiliated himself enough.

Molosov and the others stood expressionless, drawing shallow breaths, waiting for Karadzic's next move in this absurd game. An hour ago, Janjic was bored with the distraction of the village. Ten minutes ago, he found himself horrified at beating the priest. And now . . . now he was slipping into an odd state of anger and apathy drummed home by the plodding footfalls about him.

The girl with a flat face and freckles—the birthday girl dressed in pink—suddenly stood up.

She stood on the third step and stared at the commander for a few moments, as if gathering her resolve. She was going to do something. What had come over this girl? She was a *child*, for heaven's sake. A war child, not so innocent as most at such a tender age, but a child nonetheless. He'd never seen a young girl as brave as this one looked now, standing with arms at her sides, staring at the commander across the courtyard.

"Nadia!" a woman called breathlessly. Her mother, Ivena, who had stopped beneath her heavy cross.

Without removing her eyes from the commander, the girl walked down the steps and limped for Karadzic.

"Nadia! Go back! Get back on the steps this minute!" Ivena cried.

The girl ignored her mother's order and walked right up to the commander. She stopped five feet from him and looked up at his face. Karadzic didn't return her wide stare but kept his eyes fixed on some unseen point directly ahead. Nadia's eyes were misty, Janjic saw, but she wasn't crying.

It occurred to Janjic that he had stopped breathing. Sound and motion had been sucked from the courtyard as if by a vacuum. The children's whimpers fell silent. The women froze in their tracks. Not an eye blinked.

The girl spoke. "Father Michael has taught us that in the end only love matters. Love is giving, not taking. My friends were giving me gifts today because they love me. Now you've taken everything. Do you hate us?"

The commander spit at her. "Shut up, you ugly little wench! You have no respect?"

"I mean no disrespect, sir. But I can't stand to see you hurt our village."

"Please, Nadia," Ivena said.

The priest stood quivering, his face half off, his shoulders grotesquely slumped, staring at Nadia with his one good eye.

Karadzic blinked. Nadia turned to face her mother and spoke very quietly. "I'm sorry, Mother."

She looked Karadzic in the eyes. "If you're good, sir, why are you hurting us? Father Michael has taught us that religion without God is foolishness. And God is love. But how is this love? Love is—"

"Shut your hole!" Karadzic lifted a hand to strike her. "Shut your tiny hole, you insolent—"

"Stop! Please stop!" Ivena staggered forward three steps from the far side, uttering little panicky guttural sounds.

Karadzic glared at Nadia, but he did not swing his hand.

Nadia never took her round blue eyes off the commander. Her lower lip quivered for a moment. Tears leaked down her cheeks in long, silent streams. "But, sir, how can I shut up if you make my mother carry that load on her back? She has only so much strength. She will drop the cross, and then you'll beat her. I can't stand to watch this."

Karadzic ignored the girl and looked around at the scattered women, bent, unmoving, staring at him. "March! Did I tell you to stop? March!"

But they did not. Something had changed, Janjic thought. They looked at Karadzic, their gazes fixed. Except for Ivena. She was bent like a pack mule, shaking, but slowly, ever so slowly, she began to straighten with the cross on her back.

Janjic wanted to scream out. *Stop, woman! Stop, you fool! Stay down!*

Nadia spoke in a wavering tone now. "I beg you, sir. Please let these mothers put down their crosses. Please leave us. This would not please our Lord Jesus. It's not his love."

"Shut up!" Karadzic thundered. He took a step toward Nadia, grabbed one of her pigtails, and yanked.

She winced and stumbled after him, nearly falling except for his grip on her hair. Karadzic pulled the girl to the father, who looked on, tears running down his cheek now.

Ivena's cross slipped from her back then.

Janjic alone watched it, and he felt its impact through his boot when it landed.

Nadia's mother ran for Karadzic. She'd already taken three long strides when the dull *thump* jerked the commander's head toward her. She took two more, half the distance to the commander, head bent and eyes fixed, before uttering a sound. And then her mouth snapped wide, and she shrieked in fury. A full-throated roaring scream that met Janjic's mind like a dentist's drill meeting a raw nerve.

Karadzic whipped the girl behind him like a rag doll. He stepped forward and met the rushing woman's face with his fist. The blow sent her reeling, bleeding profusely from the nose. She slumped to her knees, silenced to a moan.

And then another cross fell.

And another, and another, until they were slamming to the concrete in a rain of stone. The women struggled to stand tall, all of them.

Janjic thought he saw a streak of fear cross Karadzic's gray eyes. But he wasn't thinking too clearly just now. He was trembling under the weight of the atmosphere. A thick air of insanity laced with the crazy notion that *he* should stop this. That he should scream out in protest, or maybe put a bullet in Karadzic's head—anything to end this madness.

The commander jerked his pistol from his belt and shoved it against the priest's forehead. He spun the girl toward the priest and released her. "You think your dead Christ will save your priest now?"

"Sir . . ." The objection came from Janjic's throat before he could stop it.

*Stop, Janjic! Shut up! Sit back!*

But he did not. He took a single step forward. "Sir, please. This is enough. Please, we should leave these people alone."

Karadzic shot him a furious stare, and Janjic saw hatred in those deep-set eyes. The commander looked back at the girl, who was staring up at the priest through the pools of tears that rimmed her eyes.

"I think I'll shoot your priest. Yes?"

Father Michael gazed into the little girl's face. There was a connection between their eyes, shafts of invisible energy. The priest and the girl were speaking, Janjic thought. Speaking with this look of love. Tears streamed down their cheeks.

Janjic felt a wedge of panic rise to his throat. "Please, sir. Please show them kindness. They have done nothing."

"Sometimes love is best spoken with a bullet," Karadzic said.

The girl stared into the eyes of her priest, and her look gripped Janjic with terror. He wanted to tear his gaze away from the girl's face, but he couldn't. It was a look of love in its purest form, Janjic knew, a love he had never seen before.

Nadia spoke softly, still staring at the priest. "Don't kill my priest." Her voice whispered across the courtyard. "If you have to kill someone, then kill me instead."

A murmur ran though the crowd. The girl's mother clambered to unsteady legs, gulping for air. Her face twisted in anguish. "Oh God! Nadia! Nadia!"

Nadia held up a hand, stopping her mother. "No, Mother. It will be okay. You will see. It's what Father Michael has taught us. Shh. It's okay. Don't cry."

Oh, such words! From a child! Janjic felt hot tears on his cheek. He took another step forward. "Please, sir, I beg you!" It came out like a sob, but he no longer cared.

Karadzic's lips twitched once. Then again, to a grin. He lowered his gun from the priest. It hung by his waist.

He lifted it suddenly and pressed the barrel to the girl's head.

The mother's restraint snapped, and she launched herself at the commander, arms forward, fingernails extended like claws, shrieking. This time the second in command, Molosov, anticipated her move. He was running from his position behind Janjic as soon as Ivena moved, and he landed a kick to her midsection before she reached Karadzic. She doubled over and retched. Molosov jerked the woman's arms behind her and dragged her back.

Nadia closed her eyes, and her shoulders began to shake in a silent sob.

"Since your flock has failed to prove its faith, you will renounce your faith, Priest. Do that, and I will let this little one live." Karadzic's voice cut through the panic. He looked around at the women. "Renounce your dead Christ, and I will leave you all."

Ivena began to whimper with short, squeaky sounds that forced their way past white lips. For a moment the rest seemed not to have heard. Father Michael stiffened. For several long seconds his face registered nothing.

And then it registered everything, knotting up impossibly around his shattered cheekbone. His tall frame began to shake with sobs, and his limp arm bounced loosely.

"Speak, Priest! Renounce Christ!"

# CHAPTER NINE

MARCI STARED at Eve, unable to tear her eyes free. At any other time, if anyone had told her that she would be so affected, so completely taken in by an old lady telling a story about soldiers playing games with a priest and some women in the war, she would have rolled her eyes.

But there was something about this story that had put talons into her heart and refused to let go. She was having a hard time breathing, and her heart was pounding loudly enough for anyone in the room to hear.

Something was happening to her. She was almost certain that she knew who she was in the story, but she couldn't bring herself to admit it. Not yet.

She could hear the priest's song, and she could see the field, and she was sure that what Father Michael was seeing was real, and not just in his mind. But none of that made sense, because it *was* just a story.

Or was it?

It didn't feel like just a story. The world Father Michael was seeing didn't feel like a fantasy. In that world he was beautiful, and the children were beautiful, but he was the only one who could see into that world.

Except Marci. She could see into the world right now. Not with her eyes, but with her mind's eye. But it was real.

For that matter, her own life was no more real. It was just a story, in some ways. Filled with pain and her own kind of suffering.

Eve was reading. Marci shifted in her chair and carefully wiped her sweaty palms on her red plaid skirt.

FATHER MICHAEL'S world kept blinking on and off, alternating like intermittent static between this ghastly scene here and the white-flowered field there. He was jerked back and forth with such intensity that he hardly knew which scene was real and which was a figment of his imagination.

But that was just it. Neither world came from his imagination. He knew that now with certainty. He was simply being allowed to see and hear both worlds. His spiritual eyes and ears were being opened in increments, and he could hardly stand the contrast. One second this terrifying evil in the courtyard, and the next the music.

Oh, the music! Impossible to describe. Raw energy stripping him of all but pleasure. The man was only a few hundred meters distant now, arms spread so that his cloak draped wide. An image of Saint Francis, but more. Yes, much more. Michael imagined a wide, mischievous grin on the man, but he couldn't see it for the distance. The man walked toward him steadily, purposefully, still singing. The giggling children sang with him in perfect harmony now. A symphony slowly swelling. The melody begged him to join. To leap into the field and throw his arms up and dance with laughter along with the hidden children.

Across the courtyard, the tall cross leading to the cemetery stood bold against the other world's gray sky. He had pointed to that very cross a thousand times while teaching his children the truth of God. And he had taught them well.

"You may look at that cross and think of it as a gothic decoration, engraved with roses and carved with style, but do not forget that it represents life and death. It represents the scales on which all of our lives will be weighed. It's an instrument of torture and death—the symbol of our faith. They butchered God on a cross. And Christ emphasized none of his teachings so adamantly as our need to take up our own crosses and follow him."

Nadia had looked up to him, squinting in the sun—he saw it

79

clearly in his mind's eye now. "Does this mean that we should die for him?"

"If need be, of course, Nadia. We will all die, yes? So then if we have worn out our bodies in service to him, then we are dying for him, yes? Like a battery that expends its power."

"But what if the battery is still young when it dies?" That had silenced those gathered.

He reached down and stroked her chin. "Then you would be fortunate enough to pass this plain world quickly. What waits beyond is the prize, Nadia. This"—he looked up and drew a hand across the horizon—"this fleeting world may look like the Garden of Eden to us, but it's nothing more than a taste. Tell me"—and he looked at the adults gathered now—"at a wedding feast you receive gifts, yes? Beautiful, lovely gifts . . . vases and perfumes and scarves . . . all delightful in our eyes. We all gather around the gifts and show our pleasure. 'What a glorious scarf, Ivena.'"

A chuckle ran through the crowd.

"But do you think that Ivena's mind is on the scarf?" A run of giggles. "No, I think not. Ivena's mind is on her groom, waiting breathlessly in the next room. The man whom she will wed in sweet union. Yes?"

"I don't recall seeing a cross at the last wedding," Ivena had said.

"No, not at our weddings. But death is like a wedding." The crowd hushed. "And the crucifixion of Christ was a grand wedding announcement. This world we now live in may indeed be a beautiful gift from God, but do not forget that we wait with breathless anticipation for our union with him beyond this life." He let the truth finger its way through their minds for a moment. "And how do you suppose we arrive at the wedding?"

Nadia answered. "We die."

He looked down into her smiling blue eyes. "Yes, child. We die."

"Then why shouldn't we just die now?" Nadia asked.

"Heaven forbid, child! What bride do you know who would take her own life before the wedding? No one who understands how beautiful the bride is could possibly take her life before the wedding! It is perhaps the ugliest thing of all. We will all cross the threshold when the Groom calls. Until then, we wait with breathless anticipation."

One of the women had sighed with approval.

Somehow, looking at the large concrete cross now did not engender any such mirth. He looked down at the child and felt as though a shaft had been run through his heart.

*Nadia, oh my dear Nadia, what are you doing? I love you so, young child. I love you as though you were my own. And you are my own. You know that, don't you, Nadia?*

She looked at him with deep blue eyes. *I love you, Father.* Her eyes were speaking to him, as clearly as any words. And he wept.

"Don't kill my priest. If you have to kill someone, then kill me instead," a voice said.

He heard the words like a distant echo . . . words! She had actually said that? *Don't be foolish, Nadia!*

A flash of light sputtered to life about him. The white field again!

The music flooded his mind, and he suddenly wanted to laugh with it. It felt so . . . consequential here, and the silly little game back in the courtyard so . . . petty. Like a game of marbles with all the neighborhood children gathered, sporting stern faces as if the outcome might very well determine the fate of the world. If they only knew that their little game felt so small here, in this immense white landscape that rippled with laughter. Ha! If they only knew! Kill us! Kill us all! Put an end to this silly game of marbles and let us get on with life, with laughing and music in the white field.

The white world blinked off. But now the commander had the gun pushed against Nadia's forehead. "Renounce your faith, Priest and I will let this little one live! Renounce your dead Christ, and I will leave you all."

It took a moment for him to switch worlds—for the words to present their meaning to him.

And then they did with the force of a sledge to his head.

*Renounce Christ?*

Never! He could never renounce Christ!

*Then Nadia will die.*

This realization cut through his bones like a dagger. She would die because of him! His face throbbed with pain; the muscles there

82

had gone taut like bowstrings. But never! Never could he renounce his love for Christ!

Father Michael had never before felt the torment that descended upon him in that moment. It was as if some molten hand had reached into his chest and grabbed hold, searing frayed nerves so that he could not draw breath. His throat pulled for air to no avail.

*Nadia! Nadia! I can't!*

"Speak, Priest! Renounce Christ!"

She was crying. Oh, the dear girl was crying! The courtyard waited.

The music filled his mind.

Fresh air flooded his lungs. Relief, such sweet relief! The white field ran to the horizon; the children laughed incessantly.

"I will count to three, Priest!"

The commander's voice jerked him back to the courtyard.

Nadia was looking at him. She had stopped her crying. Sorrow overcame him again.

"One!" Karadzic barked.

"Nadia," Father Michael croaked. "Nadia, I—"

"Don't, Father," she said softly. Her small pink lips clearly formed the words. *Don't, Father.* Don't what? This from a child! Nadia, dear Nadia!

"Two!"

A wail rose over the crowd. It was Ivena. Poor Ivena. She strained against the large soldier who held her arms pinned behind her back. She clenched her eyes and dropped her jaw and now screamed her protest from the back of her throat. The soldier clamped a hand around her face, stifling her cry.

*Oh God, have mercy on her soul! Oh God . . .* "Nadia . . ." Father Michael could barely speak, so great was the pressure in his chest. His legs wobbled beneath him, and suddenly they collapsed. He landed on his knees and lifted his one good arm to the girl. "Nadia—"

"I heard the song, Father." She spoke quietly. Light sparkled through her eyes. A faint smile softened her features. The girl had lost her fear. Entirely!

Nadia hummed, faint, high-pitched, clear for all to hear. "Hm hm hm hmhmm . . ."

*The melody! Dear God, she heard it too!*

"Three!" Karadzic barked.

"I saw you there," she said. And she winked.

Her eyes were wide open, an otherworldly blue penetrating his, when the gun bucked in the commander's thick, gnarled hand.

*Boom!*

Her head snapped back. She stood in the echoing silence for an endless moment, her chin pointed to the sky, baring that tender, pale neck. And then she crumpled to the ground like a sack of potatoes— a small one wrapped in a pink dress.

Father Michael's mind began to explode. His own voice joined a hundred others in a long epitaph of distress. "Aaaaahhhhhh . . ." It screamed past his throat until the last whisper of breath had left his lungs. Then it began again, and Michael wanted desperately to die. He wanted absolutely nothing but to die.

Ivena's mouth lay wide open, but no sound came out. Only a breath of terror that seemed to strike Michael on his chest.

The priest's world began to spin, and he lost his orientation. He fell forward, face first, swallowed by the horror of the moment. His head struck the concrete, and his mind began to fade. Maybe he was in hell.

# CHAPTER TEN

EVE WAS reading through tears now, wiping at her eyes with the back of her hand, and sniffing, and trying to keep the page clear enough to read. The sorrow—a deep, healing balm—washed through her chest in relentless waves.

*Do this in remembrance of me.*

Marci sat in her chair like a rag doll, struggling to maintain her last ties to self-restraint. Tears streamed down her cheeks, and her lips quivered.

*She is changing,* Eve thought.

If she wasn't mistaken, Marci was playing the part of Nadia. But Nadia's part wasn't over, was it? Not even close.

*Hold on, dear Marci. Just hold on. Everything will turn out; you'll see. The best is yet to come.*

Eve's fingers trembled as she turned the page. The pages were worn ragged on the corners. In every truly life-changing story is a mountain that rises to the heavens. But before the mountain is a valley that descends into the depths. In all honesty, Eve didn't know whether Nadia's death was a mountain or a valley. It really depended on perspective.

And truly, the perspective was about to change.

JANJIC STARED, his eyes wide and stinging. All about him voices of torment screamed; pandemonium erupted on the courtyard floor. Father Michael lay facedown, his head not five inches from the girl's shiny white birthday shoes.

Karadzic reached out and snatched another child by the collar. The boy's mother wailed in protest, started forward, and then stopped when Karadzic shoved the gun toward her. "Shut up! Shut up! Everyone!" he thundered.

Janjic was running before his mind processed the order to run. Straight for the priest. Or perhaps straight for Karadzic; he didn't know which until the last possible second. The man had to be stopped.

How the commander managed to get his pistol around so quickly, Janjic had no clue, but the black Luger whipped around and met him with a jarring blow to his cheek.

Pain shot through his skull. He felt as if he'd run into a swinging bat. His head jerked back, and his legs flew forward, throwing him from his feet. Janjic landed heavily on his back and rolled over, moaning. What was he doing? Stopping Karadzic—that's what he was doing.

Janjic dragged himself from the commander, urged by a boot kick to his thigh. His mind swam. The world seemed to slow. Five feet away on the ground lay a girl who'd just given her life for her priest. For her God. For Christ's love. And Janjic had seen in her eyes a look of absolute certainty. He had seen her smile at the priest. He had seen the wink. A *wink*, for goodness' sake! Something had changed with that wink. He was not sure what it meant, except that something had changed.

*Dear God, she had hummed! She had winked!*

"Puzup, get him to his feet," Karadzic ordered above the din.

Puzup stormed past Janjic and yanked the priest to his feet. Paul gaped at the scene, his expression impossible to interpret. Janjic pushed himself to his knees, ignoring the pain that throbbed through his skull. Blood dripped to the concrete from a wound behind his ear. He turned back to the commander and stood shakily. Ten feet separated them now.

The priest wavered on his feet, facing Karadzic. If the father had passed out from his fall, they had awakened him. The little boy the commander had hauled from the steps stood shaking and bawling. Karadzic pressed his pistol against the boy's ear.

"What do you say, Priest? What's this love of yours worth? Should I put another one of your children out of their misery?" Karadzic's eyes were rocks behind bushy brows, dull gray tombstones. He was grinning. "Or will you renounce your stupid faith?"

"Kill me," Father Michael's voice quavered.

Janjic stopped trying to understand the madness that had gripped this priest and his flock of sheep. It was beyond the reaches of his mind. Yet it reached out to him with long fingers of desire.

"Take my life, sir. Please leave the boy."

The smile vanished from the commander's face. "Then renounce your faith, you blithering idiot! They are words! Just words! Say them. Say them!"

"They are words of Christ. He is my Redeemer. He is my Savior. He is my Creator. How can I deny my own Creator? Please, sir—"

"He is your redeemer? He is her redeemer too?" He motioned to the girl on the ground. "She is dead, you fool."

The priest stood trembling for a few moments before responding. "She sees you now. She is laughing."

Karadzic stared at Father Michael.

The women had stopped their cries, and the children sat still, their faces buried in their mothers' skirts.

"If you must have another death, let it be mine," the priest said.

And then the rules of the game changed once more.

The girl's mother, Ivena, who had grown eerily calm, suddenly wrested herself free from Molosov but did not rush the commander again. Molosov grabbed one arm but let her stand on her own.

"No," she said softly, "let it be mine. Kill me in the boy's place." She stood unflinching, like a stone statue.

Karadzic now stood with the pistol to the whimpering boy's ear, between a man and a woman each asking for death in the boy's place. He shifted on his feet, unsure how much power he truly held over this scene.

Another woman stepped forward, her face twisted in pity. "No. No, kill me instead. I will die for the boy. The priest has already suffered too much. And Ivena has lost her only child. I am childless. Take my life. I will join Nadia."

"No, I will," another said, taking two steps forward. "You are young, Kota. I am old. Please, this world holds no appeal for me. It would be good for me to pass on to be with our Lord." The woman looked to be in her fifties.

Karadzic slashed the air with his pistol. "Silence! Perhaps I should kill *all* of you! I am killing here, not playing a game. You want me to kill you all?"

Janjic had known the man long enough to recognize his faltering. But something else was there as well. A glimmer of excitement that flashed through his gray eyes. Like a dog in heat.

"But it really should be me," a voice said. Janjic looked to the steps where another girl stood facing them with her heels together.

"Nadia was my best friend," she said. "I should join her. Is there really music there, Father?"

The priest could not answer. He was weeping uncontrollably. Torn to shreds by this display of love.

The gun boomed and Janjic flinched.

Karadzic held the weapon above his head. He'd fired into the air. "Stop! Stop!" He shoved the boy sprawling to his seat. His thick lips glistened with spittle. The gun shook in his thick fingers, and above it all, his eyes sparkled with rising excitement.

He stepped back and turned the pistol on Nadia's mother. She simply closed her eyes. Janjic understood her motivation to some degree: the woman's only child lay at her feet. She was stepping up to the bullet with a grief-ravaged mind.

He held his breath in anticipation of a shot.

Karadzic licked his wet lips and jerked the weapon to the younger woman who'd stepped forward. She, too, closed her eyes. But Karadzic did not shoot. He swiveled it to the older woman. Looking at them all now, Janjic thought that any one of the women might give her life for the boy. It was a moment that could not be understood in the context of normal human experience. A great spiritual love had settled on them all. Karadzic was more than capable of killing; he was, in fact, eager for it. And yet the women stood square shouldered now, daring him to pull the trigger.

Janjic swayed on weak legs, overcome by the display of self-sacrifice. The ravens cawed overhead, and he glanced skyward, as much for a reprieve as in response to the birds' call. At first he thought the ravens had flown off, that a black cloud had drifted over the valley in their place. But then he saw the cloud ebb and flow, and he knew it was a singular ring of birds—a hundred or more, gliding overhead, making their odd call. What was happening here? He lowered his eyes to the courtyard and blinked against the buzz that had overtaken the pounding in his skull.

For a long, silent minute, Karadzic weighed his decision, his muscles strung to the snapping point, sweating profusely, breathing heavily.

The villagers did not move; they drilled him with steady stares. The priest seemed to float in and out of consciousness, swaying on his feet, opening and closing his eyes periodically. His face drifted through a range of expressions—one moment his eyes open and his mouth sagging with grief, the next his eyes closed and his mouth open in wonder. Janjic studied him, and his heart broke for the man. He wanted to take the gentle priest to a bed and dress his wounds. Bathe him in hot water and soothe his battered shoulder. His face would never be the same; the damage looked far too severe. He would probably be blind in his right eye, and eating would prove difficult for some time. Poor priest. *My poor, poor priest. I swear that I will care for you, my priest. I will come and serve* . . .

What was this? What was he thinking? Janjic stopped himself. But it was true. He knew it then as much as he had known anything. He loved this man. He cherished this man. His heart felt sick over this man.

. . . *I will come and serve you, my priest.* A knot rose in Janjic's throat, suffocating him. *In you, I have seen love, Priest. In you, and your children, and your women, I have seen God. I will . . .*

A chuckle interrupted his thoughts. The commander was chuckling. Looking around and chuckling. The sound engendered terror. The man was completely mad! He suddenly lowered his gun and studied the crowd, nodding slightly, tasting a new plan on his thick tongue.

"Haul this priest to the large cross," he said. No one moved. Not even Molosov, who stood behind Ivena.

"Are you deaf, Molosov? Take him. Puzup, Paul, help Molosov." He stared at the large stone cross facing the cemetery. "We will give them what they desire."

FATHER MICHAEL remembered stumbling across the concrete, shoved from behind, tripping to his knees once, and then being hauled up under his arms. He remembered the pain shooting through his shoulder and thinking someone had pulled his arm off. But it still swung ungainly by his side.

He remembered the cries of protest from the women. "Leave the father! I beg you . . . He's a good man . . . Take one of us. We beg you!"

The world twisted topsy-turvy as they approached the cross. They left the girl lying on the concrete in a pool of blood. *Nadia . . . Nadia, sweet child.* Ivena knelt by her daughter, weeping bitterly again, but a soldier jabbed her with his rifle, forcing her to follow the crowd to the cemetery.

The tall stone cross leaned against a white sky, gray and pitted. It had been erected a hundred years earlier. They called it stone, but the twelve-foot cross was actually cast of concrete, with etchings of rosebuds at the top and at the beams' intersection. Each end flared like a clover leaf, giving the instrument of death an incongruous sense of delicacy.

The pain on his right side reached to his bones. Some had been broken. *Oh Father. Dear Father, give me strength.* The dove still sat on the roof peak and eyed them carefully. The spring bubbled without pause, oblivious of this treachery.

They reached the cross, and a sudden brutal pain shot through Michael's spine. His world faded.

When his mind crawled back into consciousness, a wailing greeted him. His head hung low, bowed from his shoulders, facing the dirt. His ribs stuck out like sticks beneath stretched skin. He was naked except for white boxer shorts, now stained with sweat and blood.

Michael blinked and struggled for orientation. He tried to lift his head, but pain sliced through his muscles. The women were singing—long, mournful wails without tune. Mourning for whom? *For you. They're mourning you!*

But why? It came back to him then. He had been marched to the cross. They had lashed him to the cross with a hemp rope around the midsection and shoulders, leaving his feet to dangle free.

He lifted his chin slowly and craned for a view, ignoring the shafts of pain down his right side. The commander stood to his left, the barrel of his pistol confronting Michael like a small black tunnel. The man looked at the women, most of whom had fallen to their knees, pleading with him.

A woman's words came to Michael. "He's our priest. He's a servant of God. You cannot kill him! You cannot." It was Ivena.

*Oh dear Ivena! Your heart is spun of gold!*

The priest felt his body quiver as he slowly straightened his heavy head. He managed to lift it upright and let it flop backward. It struck the concrete cross with a dull thump.

The wailing ceased. They had heard. But now he stared up at the darkened sky. A white, overcast sky filled with black birds. *Goodness, there must be hundreds of birds flying around up there.* He tilted his head to his left and let it loll so that it rested on his good shoulder.

Now he saw them all. The kneeling women, the children staring with bulging eyes, the soldiers. Their commander looked up at him and smiled. He was breathing heavily; his gray eyes were bloodshot. A long, thin trail of spittle ran down his chin and hung suspended from a wet chin. He was certifiably mad, this one. Mad or possessed.

The lunatic turned back to the women. "One of you. That's all! One, one, one! A single stray sheep. If *one* of you will renounce Christ, I will leave you all!"

Father Michael felt his heart swell in his chest. He looked at the women and silently pleaded for them to remain quiet, yet he doubted his dismay showed—his muscles had lost most of their control.

*Do not renounce our Lord! Don't you dare speak out for me! You cannot take this from me!*

He tried to speak, but only a faint groan came out. That and a string of saliva, which dripped to his chest. He moved his eyes to Ivena. *Don't let them, Ivena. I beg you!*

"What's wrong with you? You can't hear? I said *one* of you! Surely you have a sinner in your pretty little town willing to speak out to save your precious priest's miserable neck! Speak!"

Bright light filled Michael's mind, blinding him to the cemetery.

The field! But something had changed. Silence!

Absolute silence.

The man had stopped, thirty meters off, legs planted in the flowers, hands on his hips, dressed in a robe like a monk. Above his head, the light still streaked in from the horizon. And silence.

Michael blinked. What . . .

*Sing, O son of Zion; Shout, O child of mine;*
*Rejoice with all your heart and soul and mind.*


The man's words echoed over the field.

*Child of mine!* Michael's lips twitched with a slight grin. *Rejoice with all . . .*

The man suddenly threw out his arms to either side, lifted his head to the sky, and sang.


*Every tear you cried dried in the palm of my hand;*
*Every lonely hour was by my side.*
*Every loved one lost, every river crossed,*
*Every moment, every hour was pointing to this day,*
*Longing for this day . . .*
*For you are finally home.*


Michael felt as though he might faint for the sheer power of the melody. He wanted to run to the man. He wanted to throw out his own arms and tilt back his head and wail the same song from the bottom of his chest. A few notes dribbled past Michael's lips, uncontrolled. "La da da da la . . ."

A faint giggling sound came from his left. He turned.

She was skipping toward him in long bounds. Michael caught his breath. He could not see her face, because the girl's chin was tilted back so that she stared at the sky. She leaped through the air, landing barefoot on the white petals every ten yards, her fists pumping with each footfall. Her pink dress fluttered in the wind.

She was echoing the man's melody now, not like Michael had done, but perfectly in tune and then in harmony.

Father Michael knew then that this girl hurtling toward him was Nadia. And in her wake followed a thousand others, bubbling with a laughter that swelled with the music.

The song swallowed him whole now. They were all singing it, led by the man. It was impossible to discern the laughter from the music—they were one and the same.

Nadia lowered her head and shot him a piercing stare as she flew by. Her blue eyes sparkled mischievously, as though daring him to give chase.

But there was a difference about Nadia. Something so startling that Michael's heart skipped a beat.

Nadia was beautiful!

She looked exactly as she had before her death. Same freckles, same pigtails, same plump facial features. But in this reality he found that those freckles and that thick face and all that had made her homely before now looked . . .

Beautiful. Nearly intoxicating. His own perspective had changed! He took an involuntary step forward, dumbfounded. And he knew in that moment that his pity for both Nadia's appearance and her death had been badly misplaced.

Nadia was beautiful all along. Physically beautiful. And her death held its own beauty as well.

*Oh death, where is thy sting?*

For the first time, his eyes saw her as she truly was. Before, his sight had been masked by a preoccupation with the reality that now seemed foolish and distant by comparison. Like mud pies next to delicious mounds of ice cream.

A wind rushed by, filled with the laughter of a thousand souls. The white flower petals swirled in their wake. Michael couldn't hold back his chuckles now. They shook his chest.

"Nadia!" he called. "Nadia."

She disappeared over the horizon. He looked out to the man.

Gone!

But the voice still filled the sky. Michael's bones felt like putty. Nothing else mattered now. Nothing.

They suddenly came at him again, streaking in from the left, led by this beautiful child he'd once thought was ugly. This time she had her head down. She drilled him with sparkling, mischievous eyes while she was still far off.

He wanted to join her train this time. To leap out in its wake and fly with her. He was planning to do just that. His whole body was quivering for this intoxicating ride that she was daring him to take.

The desire flooded his veins, and he staggered forward a step.

He staggered! He did not fly as she flew!

Nadia rushed up to him, then veered skyward with a single leap. His mouth dropped open. She shot for the streaking light above. Her giggles rose to a shrieking laughter, and he heard her call, crystal clear.

"Come on, Father Michael! Come on! You think this is neat? This is *nothing*!"

It reverberated across the desert. *This is nothing!*

*Nothing!*

Desperation filled Michael. He took another step forward, but his foot seemed filled with lead. His heart slammed in his chest, flooding his veins with fear. "Nadia! Nadia!"

The white field turned off as if someone had pulled a plug.

Michael realized that he was crying. He was back in the village, hanging on a cross before his parishioners . . . crying like a baby.

# CHAPTER ELEVEN

"IT'S ME!"

Marci slipped out of her chair and dropped to her knees with a soft *thump,* face wrinkled, hands wringing her skirt.

"I'm Nadia!"

Eve dropped the book in her lap. In reality, Marci could have said Janjic or Father Michael, and it wouldn't have mattered. What did matter was that she'd entered the story, mind, heart, and soul.

"It's real." Marci said. "I'm Nadia."

"You're flying through the sky, laughing hysterically," Eve said. "Look at your hand."

Marci lowered her eyes and stared at her chubby fingers.

"You see, like Nadia's hand. In truth—in the reality that's more real than most know—your hand is beautiful. Physically beautiful, to the eye opened by the truth. I told you it wasn't inner beauty." Eve smiled.

"But I don't *care* about beauty! It feels horrible to care about beauty now."

"No, child. Nadia was beautiful. Is beautiful. Her death itself was beautiful in its own way. The story turns everything on its head, but don't dismiss the loveliness of beauty. Just understand that you, too, are beautiful."

Marci stared up at her, eyes wide. She understood.

"Everyone's Nadia?"

"Perhaps. Some are Father Michael. Most are Janjic. Some of us are Ivena."

Tears streamed down Marci's face.

Eve set down the book and eased herself to her knees in front of the girl. "I'm so sorry, dear child." She put a hand on Marci's cheek. "There's more to the . . ."

Marci let out a huge sob and threw her arms around Eve. "I'm sorry!"

"Shhh . . . shhh. It's okay."

"You're her, aren't you? You're Ivena. You're Nadia's mother." Marci held her tight. "I'm sorry. I'm so sorry, Ivena."

Their roles were suddenly reversed. Marci was now the comforter, and Eve the grieving mother. Because it was true; she really was Ivena. She couldn't stop herself from weeping on Marci's shoulder.

"That's what some people call me, yes."

To her close friends she was still Ivena. To most she was still Ivena, because most of her friends were close.

They held each other for several long minutes, flying in Nadia's world, Father Michael's world, the world of the martyr's song, the real world behind the skin of this world, where everything really is beautiful.

"Tell me the rest," Marci said. "Please, I need to know how it ends."

"It doesn't end. We're part of the story today even. It'll never end."

"Then tell me what happened to Father Michael. To Janjic. To . . . to you."

Ivena kissed her on the cheek, returned to her chair, picked up the book, sniffed once, and read.

JANJIC WATCHED the priest's body heaving with sobs up on that cross, and he pushed himself unsteadily to his feet. Nothing mattered to him now except that the priest be set free. If need be, he would die, or kill, or renounce Christ himself.

But with a single look into the priest's eyes, Janjic knew the priest wanted to die now. He'd found something of greater value than life. He had found this love for Christ.

Karadzic was shaking his gun at the priest, glaring at the villagers, trying to force apostasy, and carrying on as if he thought the whole thing was some delicious joke. But the priest had led his flock well.

They didn't seem capable of speaking out against their Christ, regardless of what it meant to the priest.

"Speak now or I'll kill him!" Karadzic screamed.

"I will speak."

Janjic lifted his head. Who'd said that? A man. The priest? No, the priest did not possess the strength.

"I will speak for my children." It *was* the priest! It was the priest, lifting his head and looking squarely at Karadzic as if he'd received a transfusion of energy.

"Your threat of death doesn't frighten us, Soldier." He spoke gently, without anger, through tears that still ran down his face. "We've been purchased by blood; we live by the power of that blood; we will die for that blood. And we would never, never renounce our beloved Christ." His voice croaked. "He is our Creator, sir."

The priest turned his eyes to the women, and slowly a smile formed on his cracked lips. "My children, please. Please . . ." His face wrinkled with despair. His beard was matted with blood, and he could hardly speak for all the tears now.

"Please." The priest's voice came softly now. "Let me go. Don't hold me back . . . Love all those who cross your path; they are all beautiful. So . . . so very beautiful."

Not a soul moved.

A cockeyed, distant smile crossed the priest's lips. He lowered his head, exhausted. A flutter of wings beat through the air. It was the white dove flapping toward them. It hovered above the father, then settled quietly on the cross, eyeing the bloodied man three feet under its stick feet.

The sound came quietly at first, like a distant train struggling up a hill. But it was no locomotive; it was the priest, and he was laughing. His head hung, and his body shook.

Janjic instinctively took a step backward.

The sound grew louder. Maybe the man had gone mad. But Janjic knew that nothing could be further from the truth. The priest was perhaps the sanest man he had ever known.

He suddenly lifted his head and spoke. No, he didn't speak; he sang. With mucus leaking from his nostrils and tears wetting his bloodied cheeks, wearing a face of unearthly delight, he threw back his head and sang in a rough, strained voice.

"Sing, O child of mine . . ."

And then he began to laugh.

The picture of contrasts slammed into Janjic's chest and took his breath away. Heat broke over his skull and swept down his back.

The silvery laughter echoed over the graveyard now. Karadzic trembled, rooted to the earth. Ivena was looking up at the priest, weeping with the rest of the women. But it was not terror or even sorrow that gripped her; it was something else entirely. Something akin to desire. Something . . .

A gunshot boomed around Janjic's ears, and he jumped. A coil of smoke rose from Karadzic's waving pistol.

The resounding report left absolute silence in its wake, snuffing out the laughter. Father Michael slumped on the cross. If he wasn't dead, he would be soon enough.

Then Janjic ran. He whirled around, aware only of the heat crashing through his body. He did not think to run; he just ran. On legs no stronger than puffs of cotton, he fled the village.

When his mind caught up to him, it told him that he also had just died.

# EPILOGUE

IVENA CLOSED the book and took a deep breath.

"That's the end?" Marci asked.

"Do you need more?" Ivena handed *The Dance of the Dead* to Marci. "I think you've heard what you need to hear for now."

"But what happened to the commander? Did he . . ." She trailed off.

"Kill the rest of us? No. He could have killed us, but Janjic had escaped the scene and could have implicated the man. Even war has its rules. And the laughter had its own effect on Karadzic."

Marci looked at the book in her hands and sniffed. "What about Janjic?"

"Janjic wrote the book in your hands. He's relived that day a thousand times. In fact, I think he's reliving it again, now, as we speak, but that's another story."

Marci glanced at the cover again. Her eyes grew round. "Janjic? He's . . . he lives here?"

"Not in this house. I'm surprised you've never heard of him. He's quite famous."

The name sparked no recognition with Marci. She rubbed her hand over the red cover and looked at the author's name. *Jan Jovic.* "Can I read this?"

"It's yours. You *must* read it."

For a long moment they sat in silence. Then Marci stood, hugging the book to her chest. She looked out the window with a glint of purpose in her eyes.

"Thank you, Ivena."

"It's the least I can do to honor my Nadia. Remember her, Marci. Keep her story close to your heart."

The message will transform your life. Do you understand?

"We're all beautiful in the eyes of heaven," she said softly. "We're all more beautiful than we can imagine. Not just inner beauty, but really."

"Yes, my dear, we really are."

And there's more I want you to promise me you'll remember the priest's words to us all."

"Which words?"

"You aren't the only one who is beautiful, Marci. They are all beautiful—every child created by God. We must love all who cross

110

our paths as if they were Nadia, because God loves them as much as he loved Nadia."

"I'll remember," Marci said. "I promise I'll remember."

"Every time you look into the eyes of a lost and lonely child, think of Nadia. That's why I came to you. I saw Nadia. When you see others, I want you to see Nadia as well."

"I will. I swear I will."

*You hate yourself because you don't think you're beautiful . . .*

*Do you believe everything can change in the space of one breath?*

*Come to my flower shop tomorrow, and I will make you beautiful.*

"I am beautiful too, Nadia," Marci whispered as if speaking holy words that could only be spoken very carefully. She stepped forward, and it felt as though she was now walking in a different world—perhaps a world similar to the reality Nadia now lived in. The reality beyond the skin of this world.

"We are all so very beautiful too."

# STUDY GUIDE

1. Do you believe your life will extend beyond the few years that you have on this earth, and if so, to what extent do you think what happens in this life affects the next life? If you believe life extends beyond the life we live here on earth, why do most people give so little thought to the afterlife?

2. How do you define true beauty? Why do you think our culture is so preoccupied with external beauty?

3. Do you think Nadia was a fool for standing up for her faith, or a wise child who knew more than most? If you had been in Nadia's shoes, what would you have done?

4. It is said that whereas martyrdom is the epitome of courage, sui-

cide is the epitome of cowardice. Describe the difference between Nadia's spirit of courage and the spirit that drives some to contemplate suicide.

5. When Nadia and Father Michael are near death, they both hear voices laughing and rejoicing. Whose voices do you think they are hearing?

6. Jesus and most of his disciples were killed for their faith like both Nadia and Father Michael. What kind of thinking drove these people to their deaths when they had the choice to live for the sake of their loved ones by relaxing their convictions? Jesus ministered for a mere three years and died as a young man; couldn't he have done the world more good by living longer?

7. In cosmic terms, every person dies very soon after he or she is born, usually within eighty or so years. Who do you think live happier lives, those who cling to their lives here, or those who look forward to one day moving on? In which category would you place yourself?

8. If given the choice today, would you choose a million-dollar house, a luxury car, a wonderful spouse, and plenty of money to burn, or the invitation to join Nadia and the singer, screaming

with delight through the sky? Are you sure?

9. Are most Christians you know obsessed with heaven, or are they so enamored with life on earth that heaven is mostly an afterthought? Do you find this hypocritical? Are you hypocritical?

10. Millions die each day. If you were hit by a truck today, would this be a good thing for you or a bad thing? Explain.

Escape mundane, powerless existenc and passionately pursue God's highest pleasures.

AS BELIEVERS, OUR WALK WITH GOD IS MOTIVATED BY HOPE—not the bland, vague notion most people have, but the expectation of an exotic, pleasurable inheritance that guides us and fires our passion . . . or, at least, should.

Ted Dekker has written an exposé on the death of pleasure within the Church. Because many of us have set aside hope and the inspired imagination that drives it, Dekker says we have been lulled into a slumber of boredom, even despondency. Our faith wanes, the joy at having been liberated fades, and we feel powerless. *The Slumber of Christianity* explores what robs us of happiness and how we can rediscover it and live lives that rekindle hope. The pursuit of pleasure is a gift to all humans—a function of the Creator himself, who is bent upon our happiness.

It's time for Christians to reclaim our inheritance of pleasure. *The Slumber of Christianity* will inflame hearts toward full-fledged, mind-expanding encounters with hope, through the imagination.

### NELSON BOOKS
A Division of Thomas Nelson Publishers
*Since 1798*

www.thomasnelson.com

# JOIN THE CIRCLE

Chat with other
Ted fans, watch the
trailers for his
books and movies, and
be the first to find
out about Ted's
writer's conferences.

www.teddekker.com

# REaD TED?

- Discover Ted's other
  best-selling novels

- Show off your
  'REaD TED?' gear
  to your friends

- Read advance chapters
  of his upcoming novels

- Hear and share Ted's
  vision behind
  his stories

# www.readted.com

# SHOWDOWN

Just keep telling yourself,
**"IT'S ONLY A BOOK."**

Of all the novels Ted Dekker has ever written,
this one
## TAKES YOU FURTHER . . .
## CUTS DEEPER . . .
## PLAYS FOR KEEPS.

From the mind of Ted Dekker,
the ultimate Showdown
begins **JANUARY 2006.**

WestBow
P R E S S
A Division of Thomas Nelson Publishers
Since 1798
visit us at www.westbowpress.com

PARADISE
3 MILES

# AN EXCERT FROM SHOWDOWN

"HOW MANY children?" Marsuvees Black asked, examining his fingernails. Strange behavior for a man interviewing for such a lofty position.

"Thirty-seven," David said. "And they may only be thirteen or fourteen years old, but I wouldn't call them children. They are students, yes, but most of them already have the intelligence of a postgraduate. Believe me, you've never met anyone like them."

Black settled back in the tall leather chair and pressed his thumbs and fingers together to form a triangle. He sighed. The monk from the Nevada desert was a strange one, to be sure. But David Abraham, director of the monastery's project, had to admit that genius was often accompanied by eccentric behavior.

"Thirty-seven special children who could one day change humanity's understanding of the world," Black said. "I think I could pull myself from my desert solitude for such a noble task. Wouldn't you agree? God knows I've been in solitude for three years now."

"You'll have to take that up with God," David said. "With or without you, our project will one day change the world, I can guarantee you that."

"Then why do you need me? You're aware of my"—he hesitated—"that I'm not exactly your typical monk."

"Naturally. I would say you're hardly a monk at all. You've spent a few years atoning for rather gratuitous sins, and for that I think you possess a unique appreciation for our struggle with evil."

"What makes you think I've beaten my demons?"

"Have you?"

"Do we ever?"

"Yes, we do," David said.

"If any man has truly beaten his demons, I have. But the struggle isn't over. There are new battles every day. I don't know why you need a conflicted man like me."

David thought a moment. "I don't need you. But God might. I think he does."

Black raised an eyebrow. "No one knows, you say? No one at all?"

"Only the few who must."

"And the project is sponsored by Harvard University."

"That is correct."

David had spent months narrowing his search for the right

teacher to fill the vacant post. Marsuvees Black brought certain risks, but the job was his if he chose to take the vow of secrecy and sequester himself in the Colorado mountains with them for the next four years.

The monk stared at his fingernail again. Scratched at it. A soft smile crossed his face.

"I'll let you know," he said.

## PARADISE, COLORADO
*One year later*
*Wednesday*

THE SOUND of boots crunching into gravel carried across the blacktop while the man who wore them was still a shimmering black figure approaching the sign that read *Welcome to Paradise, Colorado. Population 450.*

Cecil Marshal shifted his seat on the town's only public bench, shaded from the hot midsummer sun by the town's only drinking establishment, and measured the stranger strutting along the road's shoulder like some kind of black-caped super hero. It wasn't just the man's black broad-brimmed hat, or his dark trench coat whipped about by a warm afternoon breeze, but the way he carried himself that made Cecil think, *Jimminy Cricket, Zorro's a-coming.*

The town sat in a small valley with forested mountains that butted up against the buildings on all four sides. One road in and the same road out. The road in descended into the valley around a curve half a mile behind the stranger. The road out was a 'snaker' that took to the back country, headed north.

Paradise was a typical small mountain town, the kind with one of most things and none of many things.

One convenience store/gas station/video store/grocery store. One bar/restaurant. One old theater that had closed its doors long ago. One church. One mechanic—Paul Bitters, who fixed broken tractors and cars in his barn a mile north of town. One of a few other establishments that hardly counted as establishments.

No hospital. No arcade. No real grocery store other than the convenience store—everyone shopped in Delta, twenty miles west. No police station, or bowling alley, or car dealer, or bike shop, or choice of cuisine . . .

The only thing there was more than none or one of was hairdressers. There were three hairdressers, one on Main Street and two who worked out of their homes, which didn't really count.

"Looks lost," Johnny Drake said.

Cecil turned to the blond boy beside him. Johnny slouched back, legs dangling off the bench, watching the stranger.

His mother, Sally Drake, had come to town after being abandoned by some worthless husband when Johnny was a baby, thirteen years earlier. Sally's father, Dillon Drake, had passed away, leaving her the house that she and Johnny now lived in.

She'd decided to stay in Paradise for the house, after unsuccessfully trying to sell it. The decision was mighty courageous, considering the scandal Sally suffered shortly after her arrival. The thought of it still made Cecil angry. As far as he was concerned, the town hadn't found its soul since. They were a sick lot, these Paradise folk. If he could speak, he would stand up in that monstrosity they called a church and say so.

But Cecil couldn't speak. He was a mute. Had been since his birth, eighty-one years ago.

Cecil turned back to the stranger, who'd left the graveled shoulder and now clacked down the middle of the road in black steel-toed cowboy boots like a freshly shoed quarter horse. Black boots, black pants, black trench coat, black hat, white shirt. A real city slicker. On foot, three miles from the nearest highway. *I'll bet he's sporting a black mustache to boot.*

Cecil dropped his eyes to the leather-bound copy of *Moby Dick* in his lap. Today he would give Johnny the book that had filled his world with wonder when he was fourteen.

He looked at the boy. Kid was growing up fast. The sweetest, biggest-hearted boy any man could ever want for a son.

Johnny suddenly gasped. He had those big light-brown eyes fixed in the direction of the city slicker, and his mouth lay open as if he'd swallowed a fly.

Cecil lifted his head and followed the boy's eyes. The black-cloaked stranger strutted down Main Street's yellow dashes now, arms swinging under the folds of a calf-length duster, silver-tipped boots stabbing the air with each step. His head turned to face Cecil and Johnny.

The brief thought that Zorro might be wearing a disguise—a Halloween mask of a skull—flashed through Cecil's mind. But this was no mask. The head jutting from the stranger's white shirt was all bone. Not a lick of skin or flesh covered the bleached jaw. It smiled at them with a wide set of pearl teeth. Two eyes stared directly at Cecil, suspended in their deep bone sockets, like the eyes down at the butcher shop in Junction: too big, too round, and never blinking.

Cecil's pulse spiked. The ghostly apparition strode on, right up the middle of the street as if it owned Paradise, like a cocky gunslinger. And then the stranger veered from his course and headed directly toward them.

Cecil felt his book drop. His hands shook in his lap like the stranger's eyes, shaking in their sockets with each step, above a grinning face full of teeth. Cecil scanned the man's body, searched for the long bony fingers. There, at the end of long black sleeves, dangling limp, the stranger's hands swung to his gait.

Flesh. Strong, bronzed, fleshy hands, curving gently with a gold ring flashing in the sun. Cecil jerked his eyes back to the stranger's face and felt an ice-cold bucket of relief cascade over his head.

The face staring at him smiled gently with a full set of lips, parted slightly to reveal white teeth. A tanned nose, small and sharp but no doubt stiff with cartilage like any other nose. A thick set of eyebrows curved above the man's glinting eyes—jet-black like the color of his shoulder-length hair.

The stranger was twenty feet from them now. Cecil clamped his mouth shut and swallowed the pooled saliva. *Did I see what I just thought I saw?* He glanced down at young Johnny. The boy still gaped. Yep, he'd seen it too.

Cecil remembered the book. He bent over and scanned the dusty boards at his feet and spotted it under the bench. He reached way down so his rump raised off the bench, steadied his tipping torso with his left hand on the boardwalk, and swung his right arm under the seat. His fingers touched the book. He clasped it with bony fingers, jerked it to safety, and shoved himself up.

When his head cleared the bench, the stranger stopped in front of them. Cecil mostly saw the black pants. A zipper and two pockets. *A crotch. A polyester crotch.* He hesitated a brief moment and lifted his head.

For a moment the man just stood there, arms hanging loosely, long hair lifting from his shoulders in the breeze, black eyes staring directly into Cecil's, lips drawn tight as if to say, *Get a grip, old fool. Don't you know who I am?*

He towered, over six foot, dressed in the spotless getup with silver flashing on his boots and around his belt like one of those country-western singers on cable. Cecil tried to imagine the square chin and high cheekbones bared of flesh, stripped dry like a skull in the desert.

He couldn't.

The stranger's eyes shifted to the boy. "Hello, my friend. Mighty fine town you have here. Can you tell me where I would find the man in charge?"

Johnny's Adam's apple bobbed. But he didn't answer. The man waited, eyebrows raised like he expected a quick answer. But Johnny wasn't answering.

The man turned back to Cecil. "How about you, old man? Can you tell me who's in charge here? The mayor? Chief of police?"

"He . . . he can't speak," Johnny said.

"That right? Well you obviously can. You may not be much to look at, but your mouth works. So speak up."

Johnny hesitated. "About what?"

The man casually slipped his right hand into the pocket of his slacks and moved his fingers as if he was playing with coins. "About fixin' things around here."

*Move on stranger. You're no good. Just move on and find some other town.* He should tell the stranger that. He should stand right up and point to the edge of town and tell the man where he should take his bones.

But Cecil didn't stand up and say anything. Couldn't. Besides, his throat was still in knots, which made it difficult to breathe much less stand up and play marshal.

"Yordon?" Johnny said.

The man in black pulled his hand from his pocket and stared at it. A translucent gel of some kind smothered his fingers, a fact that seemed to distract him for a moment. His eyes shifted to Johnny.

"Yordon?" The man began to lick the gel from his hand. "And who's Yordon?" He sucked at his fingers, cleaning them. "Now you're mute, boy? Speak up."

"The father?"

The man ran his wet fingers under his nose and drew a long breath through his nostrils. "You have to love the sweet smell of truth. Care for a sniff?"

He lowered his hand and ran it under Johnny's nose. The boy jerked away, and the man swept his hand in front of Cecil's face. Smelled musty, like dirty socks. Cecil pulled back.

"What did I tell you?" the man said, grinning. "This stuff will make you see the world in a whole new way, guaranteed."

Eyes back on Johnny. "Who else?"

Johnny stared at him.

"I said *who else?* Besides the father."

Johnny glanced at the bar, thirty yards to their right. "Maybe Steve?"

"Steve. That's the owner of the bar?" The man studied Smither's Saloon.

Cecil looked at the establishment's flaking white frontage. It needed a few coats of paint, but then so did half the buildings in Paradise. A plaque hung at an odd angle behind the swinging screen door. Faded red letters spelled *Open*. A dead neon Budweiser sign hung in one of the saloon's three windows.

"Good," the stranger said. The man took a step toward the saloon, then stopped. Turned back to the bench.

*What now?* Cecil looked up at the man's face.

The man's dark eyes were twisted down, fixed on Cecil. Crooked smile.

He suddenly lifted his arm up to his shoulder and formed a prong with two fingers, like a cobra poised to strike. Slowly, he brought the hand toward Cecil and then stopped, a foot from his face.

What on earth was the man doing? What did he think—

The stranger moved his hand closer, closer. Cecil's vision blurred and he instinctively clamped his eyes shut. Hot and cold flashes ripped up and down his spine like passing fright trains. He wanted to scream. He wanted to yell for help. *Help me, boy! Can't you see what he's doing? Help me, for heaven's sake!*

But he could do nothing more than open his mouth wide and suck in air, making little gasping sounds—*hach, hach*—like a plunger working in a toilet.

A long second crawled by. Then two. Cecil stopped sucking air and jerked his eyes open. Pink filled his vision—the fuzzy pink of two fingers hovering like a wishbone an inch from his eyes.

# THE CIRCLE TRILOGY

Book One
ISBN 0-8499-1790-5

Book Two
ISBN 0-8499-1791-3

Book Three
ISBN 0-8499-1792-1

Fleeing assailants through an alleyway in Denver late one night, Thomas Hunter narrowly escapes to the roof of an industrial building. Then a silent bullet from the night clips his head and his world goes black. When he awakes, he finds himself in an entirely different reality—a green forest that seems more real than where he was. Every time he tries to sleep, he wakes up in the other world, and soon he truly no longer knows which reality is real.

Never before has a trilogy of this magnitude—all in hardcover format—been released in an eight-month window of time. On the heels of *The Matrix* and *The Lord of the Rings* comes a new trilogy in which dreams and reality collide. In which the fate of two worlds depends on one man: Thomas Hunter.

Each book in the trilogy is also available in abridged (CD) and unabridged (CD and cassette) editions.

Discover more at TedDekker.com

# A NOVEL OF GOOD, EVIL,
# AND ALL THAT LIES BETWEEN

ISBN 0-8499-4512-7

Imagine answering your cell phone one day to a mysterious voice that gives you three minutes to confess your sin. If you don't, he'll blow the car you're driving to bits and pieces. So begins a nightmare that grows with progressively higher stakes. There's another phone call, another riddle, another three minutes to confess your sin. The cycle will not stop until the world discovers the secret of your sin.

*THR3E* is a psychological thriller that starts full tilt and keeps you off balance until the very last suspense-filled page.

This novel is also available as an abridged CD audio edition.

Discover more at TedDekker.com

# THE FUTURE CHANGES IN THE BLINK OF AN EYE . . . OR DOES IT?

ISBN 0-8499-4511-9

Seth Borders isn't your average graduate student. For starters, he has one of the world's highest IQs. Now he's suddenly struck by an incredible power—the ability to see multiple potential futures.

Still reeling from this inexplicable gift, Seth stumbles upon a beautiful woman named Miriam. Unknown to Seth, Miriam is a Saudi Arabian princess who has fled her veiled existence to escape a forced marriage of unimaginable consequences. Cultures collide as they're thrown together and forced to run from an unstoppable force determined to kidnap or kill Miriam.

An intoxicating tale set amid the shifting sands of the Middle East and the back roads of America, *Blink* engages issues as ancient as the earth itself . . . and as current as today's headlines.

Discover more at TedDekker.com

# The Blessed Child Series

### Blessed Child
by Ted Dekker and Bill Bright
ISBN 0-8499-4312-4

The young orphan boy was abandoned and raised in an Ethiopian monastery. When relief expert Jason Marker agrees to take Caleb from the monastery, they begin an incredible journey filled with intrigue and peril. Together with Leiah, a nurse who escapes to America with them, Jason discovers Caleb's stunning power. Jason and Leiah fight for Caleb's survival while the world erupts into debate over the source of his power. In the end nothing can prepare any of them for what they will find.

### A Man Called Blessed
by Ted Dekker and Bill Bright
ISBN 0-8499-4380-9

In this explosive sequel to Blessed Child, Rebecca Solomon leads a team deep into the Ethiopian desert to hunt the one man who may know the final resting place of the Ark of the Covenant.

But the man in their sights is no ordinary man. His name is Caleb, and he, too, is on a quest—to find again the love he once embraced as a child.

The fate of millions rests in the hands of these three.

Discover more at TedDekker.com